Phang's fist closed around the cobra's head, keeping the deadly fangs embedded in his palm. In one clean, swift motion, he pulled his long razor-sharp blade from the scabbard on his right side and, in a continuous swing, severed the head of the snake from its body. He swung once more, and felt a cold and then a burning pain as the blade in his right hand cleaved his left hand at the wrist, allowing the fist, still locked tightly on the head of the cobra, to fall to the floor . . .

Charter Books by Barry Sadler

CASCA:

SOLDIER OF FORTUNE

#8

BARRY SADLER

CHARTER BOOKS, NEW YORK

All characters in this book are fictitious.
Any resemblance to actual persons, living or dead,
is purely coincidental.

CASCA: SOLDIER OF FORTUNE
A Charter Book / published by arrangement with
the author

PRINTING HISTORY
Charter edition / April 1983

ISBN: 0-441-09226-8

Charter Books are published by Charter Communications, Inc.
200 Madison Avenue, New York, N.Y. 10016.
PRINTED IN THE UNITED STATES OF AMERICA

FOREWORD

These are the continuing stories of the life of the man known as Casca Longinus, the Roman legionnaire who thrust the fatal lance into the side of Jesus at the Mount of Golgotha and for that crime was condemned by Jesus to wander the earth, unable to die until the Second Coming. Some years ago Casca met a Dr. Goldman at the Eighth Field Hospital in Vietnam. There he began to tell the doctor of his odyssey through the pages of history. Over the years he has periodically met with the doctor to continue his story. There is a sympathetic relationship between the two men that enables Dr. Goldman to experience all that has happened to Casca, to feel his pain and hate, his loves and passions.

For Dr. Goldman, perhaps the strangest thing of all about his sometimes unwanted visitor is the terrible sadness of Casca's isolation. Most people think that life without end would be a blessing. But Goldman has learned through Casca that to go through the centuries never being able to stay in one place for more than a few years, watching those you care for grow old and die, never to have a child of your own blood to raise is a curse. And the words of Jesus were a constant reminder: *"Soldier, you are content with what you are, then that you shall remain until we meet again,"* condemning Casca to an existence of endless conflict, to wage battle and know the horrible suffering of endless bloodshed and war until

v

some day in the unknown future Casca would be permitted to die.

For now, we only know through Dr. Goldman that Casca still lives and walks the earth searching for his own finality, doing that which he was cursed to do: *"Fight."* This is the story of one of his more contemporary adventures. Dr. Goldman has had many letters asking about what Casca is doing now, in our time. We can't tell you where he is today, but not very long ago, shortly after Vietnam, he was involved in an episode that will be related in the following pages. Casca is not a monster or genius; he is an ordinary man trapped in an extraordinary circumstance. He is with us today and will be here long after we the readers have turned to dust.

Through him we can perhaps learn how we would have reacted under the same conditions, since we are permitted to see that which he has seen and feel all that he has felt. As Dr. Goldman has told us, Casca is all men and as man has always been (locked in an eternal struggle not only with time but also with himself). He is as modern as today and as timeless as the past. Casca is and will be for unknown centuries to come "The Eternal Mercenary," or as you shall soon see, eternity's "SOLDIER OF FORTUNE."

SOLDIER OF FORTUNE

PROLOGUE

For Casca the years since he had disappeared from the Eighth Field Hospital in Nha Trang were confusing ones. It had grown more difficult and more expensive to acquire papers. After his first meeting with Goldman, he chose to leave before he had to answer any questions about his condition. That was a circumstance he was used to. It had been fairly easy to lose himself in the thousands of faceless GIs who saturated the cities, though he was surprised that there had been no attempt to find him. He couldn't have known, of course, that his files had been destroyed by Major Goldman and Colonel Landries. As far as the hospital was concerned, he had never been brought in. Therefore, to the Army he was simply listed as "missing in action" (presumed dead).

It took a little to make contact with a man who would help him. He had befriended old Phang, the Kamserai chieftain from Cambodia, several years before. Phang made him a gift of enough money to get out of the country and reach Singapore.

Once there Casca went back into the only line of work he really knew and was qualified for, one where clients didn't ask too many questions and were content to leave you alone as long as the job was done.

It also put him into contact with people who could acquire identification papers that would stand up under close scrutiny. For the right amount of money, documents

1

could be inserted into files to prove that you were born wherever you said you were. For now his papers said that he was born in Kuala Lumpur and had the right to claim Malayan citizenship. That provided him with a valid passport and documents that enabled him to get through the morass of modern customs and emigration departments. One thing he had learned long before was that as long as you had the right papers, you would seldom be asked for any other proof.

CHAPTER ONE

Nationalist China's hatred for anything communist is exceeded only by its love and respect for money.

In the great room of a fine house in Taipei City on the island of Formosa, the capital of the last outpost for the former forces of the Kuomintang of Generalissimo Chiang Kaishek, an old man sat, his family gathered before him, his shoulders heavily burdened with impending decision.

Money, thought Lin Pao Lieh, has been the solution for so many problems in the past that perhaps it may serve again for this one.

Lin Pao sighed, weary with the responsibility of many years of serving as the head of one of the great merchant families of China. In silence, their features softened in proper deference, the lesser members of his large family waited for him to speak, waited for his decision as to the answer to a problem of family honor.

His aged eyes surveyed the room slowly, as if the answer might lie somewhere inside the four walls. His eyes rested on a prized possession, the carved figure of a bodhisattva. The physical and spiritual power, the compassion and knowledge, fairly emanated from this sculpture of a person who in some future life will become a Buddha. The sculpture itself had been made by the infamous Kuan Lin in the Sung dynasty between 960 and 1280 and had come into Lin Pao's possession through the thankful hands of a man he'd aided in fleeing the terrors of communism.

In Lin's mind, the man had been gracious to the point of foolishness, but refusing the gift might have caused the man embarrassment, and so it was his to cherish now. He studied its outstretched arm, held there in the traditional gesture of teaching, and it reminded him that his own limb must soon point to his nephew in judgment.

His eyes moved now to the west wall, landing on the original painting of doves and pear blossoms. It had been painted on paper instead of the traditional silk and was said to have inspired at least a dozen of China's most famous poets. One of them, he recalled, had written words that had brought him great comfort in times of stress. What were they? It was becoming exceedingly more difficult to remember things. Now they came: "Again the snow-scented air calls me from dreams, and again the doves on a small branch in my courtyard swell their chests with spring." Such beautiful lines, he thought.

The old eyes moved now to the silken-clad figure that knelt before him, head bowed. His decision had been made.

"Han, you bring me no joy. You were and are eternally responsible for those in your care, and you have failed." His voice, soft at first, had risen somewhat.

"You should have foreseen the necessity to depart Cambodia with your goods and family long before now. Your eagerness to make a profit from a desperate people does you no honor. You forget what it was like when we left the mainland. You were but a boy, and I carried you, the son of my brother who remained there to fight, in my arms. You and your sister were all that I carried; all else was left behind. Land, wealth . . . all that our family had gathered for over two hundred years was gone. Yet I carried you, as you are my brother's son, and family must come before all else." Lin rested for a moment and then continued.

"All that survived of our family afterward joined their few possessions together, and again we have built a name that is respected throughout all Asia. From Hong Kong to

Port Moresby, the name of Pao is respected. Now you have caused us dishonor that must, and will be, erased. You left members of our family behind while saving your miserable self and your money.'' Lin looked again to the peaceful painting of the doves, composing himself in its serenity.

"This is my judgment. You will take all that you've saved, if necessary adding to it the resources of our family, and use it to rescue those you left behind. Spend it wisely; do not be niggardly. Bring our people to me, and you will be redeemed. Fail in this matter, and the kindest fate you could enjoy would be my permission to die by your own hand.'' Lin waved his arms in a gesture of dismissal.

"Go now! Leave my eyes until you have need of my assistance in whatever plan you arrive at."

Lin Pao Lieh, scion of an ancient house of merchants, leaned back and closed his eyes. It is a burden to be so old, he thought, but if Han fails, it shall be his failure, not mine, and the honor of the house will continue.

While his family knelt around him, Lin Pao nodded as old men will do and fell asleep. The family bowed and departed silently, leaving the elder to his dreams.

For Han, the responsibility placed on him was not one that gave him peace. He knew that he had failed when he'd left Cambodia without his nephews and their children, but what could he have done? Surely the old man knew that time had been of the essence if he was to salvage anything at all. Lin's decision had been unfair as far as Han was concerned, but the old man's word was law, and Han knew that he must obey, even to the death. But for now, solutions must be found to prevent that degree of self-finalization.

Han returned to his own house and went immediately to his office. Something must be done, he thought. How to get them out? It would be futile to try bribing a Khmer Rouge official; the fanatic communists did not appreciate an honest bribe. No! The only answer was that someone would have to chance going in after them and bring them out. But who? And how? Where could he find the men for such a job?

Han racked his brain. Suddenly there came a thought. Perhaps someone in the Nationalist Chinese Army would know of a man desperate and greedy enough to attempt leading such a mission as this.

He reached for the file of names he'd brought with him from Cambodia. Quickly scanning name after name, he suddenly stopped. Ah, yes. One Major Shan of the Nationalist Chinese equivalent of   American G-2. Major Shan! An interesting man, if he remembered correctly. One who also had an appreciation of the finer things in life, but sadly, not the means to enjoy them.

"Well, Major Shan," he said aloud, "this may be a fortunate day for you . . . and for me."

He dialed the number. The phone rang, and on the other end a voice answered, informing Han that he was speaking to the main office of the Military Security and Intelligence Ministry, a dreaded branch of the government. But, he thought, so much the better.

Han addressed himself courteously to the faceless voice on the other end of the phone. One never knew to whom one might be speaking in cases like this. Best to be careful with one's manners. He asked the voice if the honorable Major Shan was available to speak to this unworthy person and apologized for interrupting the faceless voice's duty by asking such a poor favor. The voice replied in a like manner, politely, for he too was unsure of whom he was speaking to, and in a job like this, many important people called regularly. It was therefore obvious that the best way to avoid offending was to be politely correct at all times and in all matters. After all, the Chinese system had not changed so much that a lesser-ranking soldier could not be shot for not showing proper respect to his superiors. This attitude, as in the old days, served to keep people calling this number, or answering it, on their best behavior at all times. Nowhere in the government or military were people more polite and better mannered than at the security levels.

"Ah, Major Shan," said the silk-clad voice of Han. "It is so good of you to take the time to speak to me. I remember with great fondness and pleasure your brief visit to our house in Phnom Penh last year."

Shan, by means of his military position, had been the willing agent in delivering several extremely valuable art pieces from Taiwan to an anxious buyer in Singapore. The major had profited well from that journey, as both recalled, and once more politeness was the order of the day. A meeting was agreed on.

That evening the mist rolled in from the straits separating Taiwan and her people from the military giant that watched and waited across the narrow waters.

Major Shan approached Han's home in the damp night. The house was lit only by the glow of an occasional lamp. The lamps, types found only in the Orient, with a thick glow to them and the light limited to only the immediate surroundings, were currently being disturbed by an occasional moth attempting suicide by beating its brains out, continuously battering its fragile head into the globe until achieving its purpose.

Shan had taken public purveyance until he was within a few city blocks of the merchant Han's residence. Again, one never knew who was watching whom; best to take no chances. This night might prove to be very profitable, if his previous association with the merchant had been any kind of an example.

The major, an honored and highly decorated officer of the Ministry of Security, came to a stop in front of a leering devil dog and a number that said he'd arrived at the gate to Han's home. He straightened his tunic and rang the bell. The door opened immediately, and an elderly Tonkinese amah bade him to enter.

The old woman, from the northern provinces of what was once known as Cochin China, led Major Shan across a courtyard that had been considered ancient when Shan's father's father was a young man. Now with the meticulous care of the centuries devoted to maintaining this one small area it was perfect, in the manner of well raked gravel and the set of the individual rocks, placed like waiting sentinels, content that they would remain when all else had passed. There was perfection, too, in the small pond where golden carp moved lazily and the miniature trees that had seen more years than many nations ever would. He thought, For a place like this, to be able to call this garden one's own would be truly all that a man could ever desire. For to be able to call such a garden one's own, one must already have everything else that is important to a graceful life. This Han, this fat merchant, must be something more than he appears.

The old woman led Shan to an open room, faced on three sides by the most expensive calligraphy screens he'd ever seen and on the other by the exquisite ancient garden.

Han rose, dressed in white robes: white, the color of spirits and the sign of mourning and great sorrow.

Ah, thought Shan. This man has great problems, and great problems require expensive solutions.

Han bade the major sit and poured, with his own hand, the welcoming cup of rice wine. As they knelt, each sizing up the other, weighing the balance and strength that the other might possess, reminiscences followed of their first brief association.

Had the good major been pleased with their last meeting? That was good. One should always have pleasant memories. Would the honorable major be averse to performing a small service once again for this unworthy merchant who could offer nothing but his friendship and gratitude and . . . perhaps just this one small gift?

Han reached to his front and pushed toward the major a small teak chest the size of a cigar box, beautifully carved with emblems of the T'ang dynasty, its teak black with age but the gold leaf of the intertwining dragons as bright as if it had been put on this very day. Shan bowed and took a deep breath to contain his excitement and steady his hand.

With difficulty he opened the box, catching his breath suddenly and blinking his eyes in disbelief. Inside were a rainbow of gems of every color and size. Sapphires, bluer than the eyes of a White Russian prostitute, deep-colored blood-red rubies from the temples of Cambodia or perhaps even Angkor Wat, emeralds from across the sea, Ming-green and sparkling.

"Ah," breathed the major. "What service may this poor ignorant soldier perform for the great and honorable merchant?" He was performing kowtow as he would have in the old days to a prince of the court of the last Emperor of the Dragons.

No matter the service requested, the price had been agreed on and the necessity for subterfuge noted. Han wiped the nervous perspiration from his brow and explained his problem and the need to resolve it. Men! Han needed men to carry out his mission. Where could they be found? Money was no problem. What the major held in his hands was his, and all other expenses would be paid by Han himself. Could the major help this poor and desperate one?

Major Shan nodded. "Yes," he affirmed to the pleading figure of Han. "Yes, I may know just the man to perform a contract such as this for you. His background and associations fit admirably with your purposes. I have used him and his associates more than once on missions that could have proved embarrassing if any of my people were found to be involved. He's an American, or at least he had been with the American forces at the time I first met him, though he now claims Malaysian citizenship. His manner is such, that he took it upon himself to assist in the evacuation of two Vietnamese nationals just hours before the communist forces moved in. It seems that this man forced an English pilot to fly to a small field outside of Saigon, where they picked up two of his friends. One, a former South Vietnamese ranger named Van Tran Tich, and the other, a disreputable-looking savage that he calls, for some unknown reason, George. I believe he said that the latter was known as a Montagnard from the highlands, something similar to our own Taiwanese aborigines. This long-nosed American, or whatever he is, has the most excellent of qualifications for our purposes. He has been exceedingly well trained in the art of war and is an expert in most every way of changing one's way of living. Personally, he gave me the distinct impression that he had a death wish and is therefore probably condemned to live a very long and most interesting life, almost as if he had a destiny to do so. But he has many contacts in the area you wish to enter, this due to his long association with the Kamserai, the displaced Cambodian bandits who operated out of South Vietnam and conducted raids back into Cambodia for the Americans before the Yankees were allowed to enter that country themselves."

Han nodded. "Would this man be able to secure the services of enough men to ensure the success of my program?"

Shan gave him an affirmative nod. "Yes, and I believe that with my good friends in the government, we may be able to lend him some direct assistance also. As you know, kind Han, the Nationalist government is always ready to render aid to anyone who may hinder or embarrass the communists."

Han grinned knowingly. "Would the honorable and brave major be able to communicate with these disreputable ones? If so, this unworthy merchant is ready to place all the funds needed to secure the services of this man and his outlaw friends, uh . . . was it Van Tran and George?"

Major Shan agreed to perform the necessary steps to secure the services of the man he knew as Casey Romain. A weird-sounding name, almost Latin, he thought. He'd once started to ask the origin of the name, but Romain was not one to ask many questions of, and he'd hesitated.

CHAPTER TWO

Taking a long, hard pull from the mug of lukewarm Australian beer, Casey Romain wiped the foam from his mouth with the back of his heavily scarred hand. The hardest thing to find in the Orient was a good iced mug of beer. Too bad, he thought, the Americans hadn't arrived before the Limeys had taught these people to enjoy warm beer.

Casey looked across the table, smiling inwardly at the picture presenting itself there. A member of the South Vietnamese aristocracy and a Montagnard savage with his teeth filed to points, were crying in their beers because a Malayan whore had just told them a hard luck story, a story Casey had heard himself in the port of Ostia in the year of . . . Damn, how long ago had it been? For Casey Romain, time had become merely the simple movement of hands around the face of a clock or the sun's circle of the earth, a nonessential event that turned days into years and years into centuries, till the passage of time was meaningless. He tore his mind away from the past. It was unpleasant.

Well, he thought, at least the passing of time with these two idiots is never boring, to say the least. He laughed inwardly at how indignant the Englishman, Harrison, had been when he had stuck a .45 into his ear and made him fly into South Vietnam to pick up George and Van. And while Harrison still complained of the way Casey treated him, they had become good friends over the years.

It was a message from Phang that told where his friends would be waiting. Phang had the message delivered to him in K.L. by an opium dealer of long aquaintance. Once he had that, there was no way he was going to leave them behind to be picked up by the North Vietnamese. Harrison had been unlucky enough to have the only plane around that had the range to get there and back.

He had become disillusioned with the Americans when they proved to him that they were willing to let thousands of good men like George and Van, who were currently seated across the table from him, to be written out of existence, men who'd thrown their lives on the line and given their loyalty to the Americans fighting the communists, to be stabbed in the back with a "tough shit" when the chips were down. These two wouldn't have lasted ten minutes once the commies had gotten their hands on them, and Phang would have bitten off a lot of trouble if he had kept them with him. He had had to get them out, and Harrison was handy at the time. Between the four of them they had done some deals together, and Singapore was a city where something was always happening or about to happen and business deals could be made. And now it seemed that they were about to be offered another contract by the good major.

He checked his wristwatch and looked toward the door, wondering what it was that Shan had on his mind, or up his sleeve, this time. The last deal he'd offered had proved to be profitable, even if it had been risky. Singapore was one of his favorite cities, and his feet were not particularly itchy for action. He'd much rather be in K.L. drinking palm toddies, but man does not live by toddy alone. The bank account was running low, and he'd been glad to hear from the major. Shan always paid well, if somewhat reluctantly.

George and Van had started to sing a somewhat disrespectful song about Chairman Mao and a passionate water buffalo, when through the smoke, which was about twenty percent opium now, walked a mufti-clad Major Shan. He was doing his best to appear an average Chinese business-man, but the stiff, rod-up-the-ass look gave him away. The straight back said military.

Shan crossed the room, ignoring the pleadings of the vintage 1940 jukebox and its scratched strains of "Don't Be Cruel." Thrusting his way between a curtain of multi-colored beads, the right honorable Major Shan looked down upon the right dishonorable Casey Romain.

Casey raised himself to the standing position, drawing his five foot ten frame erect, his two hundred compacted pounds of muscle and scar tissue making him appear smaller than he actually was. He didn't offer his hand.

"How the hell are you, Shan?" he knew that such familiarity would piss the hell out of the officer. "And what can we do for you this time?"

Shan rolled his gaze over Romain, once again analyzing this strange American, or whatever he was, who refused to show respect for his superiors. One day, he reminded himself, he would have to do something about that; but not now. For the time being he had need of this strange man with the disquieting gaze and the slightly pockmarked face, evidence of a losing bout with acne at a tender age but now giving him a somewhat sinister cast when com-bined with steady blue eyes that looked through you as if you weren't there.

Shan shook these thoughts off, collecting himself. After all, he was the one in control here, not this barbarian and his besotted companions. Ah, Lord Buddha, he thought to himself, it is unfortunate indeed that a man of my sensibili-ties must do business with animals of this caliber. But such is business, and the garden of the merchant is not as far out of reach now as it was before.

The two men seated themselves. Shan, ignoring the two singing drunks across the table, spoke first.

"Ah, my friend, it is indeed good to see you after all these many months. I thought of you often. Have you been well?"

Casey looked long and steady at the major. By God,

we're in for it now, he thought. The wily bastard's never been this nice to us before. He must have something really crazed up his sleeve.

"Thank you for your kind concern. It is indeed an honor for you to take your valuable time into consideration of such poor men as ourselves." Casey figured he might as well play the game. "How may we be of service to you?"

Shan looked about him, ascertained that no others were within earshot, and turned back to Casey.

"I have a mission for you. A mission, if successful, that may provide you and your . . . associates with enough to live comfortably for the rest of your natural life, or in their case"—he indicated the two off-key singers—"their unnatural lives." Shan immediately regretted giving in to the temptation of the small dig at Van and George.

Casey laughed, thinking, natural life? Mine? If the major only knew. "Okay, Major. You've broken the phony front of displaying Chinese manners. Now what's the deal? Lay it all out for me, the good with the bad. Then I'll tell you if we want it or not. It won't go any further than this table if we refuse the deal. I know you're not above having some of your boys shove a banana knife in our ears one night if we talk, so since we all know the score, lay it on me."

Shan let loose a deep sigh. "Ah, perhaps it is better to deal with you barbarians in your own manner. At least it limits the amount of time that I shall have to spend in your company."

"I love you too, Major," countered Casey. "Now, shit or get off the pot and let us go back to Malaya and our women."

"Very well, it shall be as you wish. This is, as you say, the deal." Shan laid out the problem of the merchant and his abandoned family members, omitting nothing except the fact that he personally would be making a small fortune at Casey's risk. "That, my barbarian friend, is the entire deal. Will you accept the contract? If so, I will, unofficially of course, make all the resources at my disposal available to you and the men of your choice. If you succeed in this mission, I am authorized to deposit to your account the sum of two hundred thousand dollars, one half when you submit an acceptable plan and the balance upon the completion of the mission. In addition, I will supply the funding for whatever else you may need, up to one hundred thousand more and payable as required. Should you need aircraft, they shall be available to you also. Will you accept the mission?''

Casey turned his eyes to Shan, loosing a breath. He'd been correct in his assumption that this one was going to be a bitch. But the price was definitely right. He looked over at his two friends. They'd fallen asleep now, holding on to each other, George mumbling endearing comments in the Bihar dialect to Van, which, if Van had been awake and sober enough to comprehend, would have led to a bloody brawl.

He turned his eyes to Shan, nodding slowly. "Give me a week to see if I can come up with a plan of operation and see if I can make contact with any of our surviving friends in that area. You did say you could supply aircraft?'' Shan nodded in the affirmative, and Casey continued. "Okay, give me a couple of grand now to cover our expenses while here and also to cover a few small bribes that will update our input. You know, I'm sure, that not a hell of a lot of info has come out of Cambodia since the Khmer Rouge took over. They've shut that place up tighter than a well digger's ass.''

Shan nodded and removed a large envelope from his inside coat pocket. "I foresaw your acceptance and your needs, my friend. In this envelope is the sum of three thousand American dollars and the current military analysis of the Cambodian situation. I will expect to hear from you in no less than two weeks. Contact me by cable at my home. In doing so, you will use the phrase 'I hope to be

able to stop over on my way to Tokyo and visit for a day
or so.' This will indicate to me that you have decided to
take on the mission. If I receive the cable, I shall contact
you at this place no more than three days later. Is that
clear?''

CHAPTER THREE

Dawn rose slow, hot, red, and wet over the harbor of Singapore. Casey sat, rocking slowly back and forth, on the small porch outside his room. He'd spent the hours since the meeting with Shan letting his mind flow, not trying to follow any particular pattern but letting the varied thoughts and patterns mingle. This was and had always been his method of allowing his subconscious to marshal all the related experiences and knowledge he'd accumulated in the past.

Taking a long drag off his smoke, he tossed the butt over the side of the porch and into the water, watching as it floated down and landed on a pile of damp leaves, fizzling itself out. The plan came, unbidden but determined, the shape of an operational format forming in his mind. He had his direction, and he knew which way to go. The problem now was to see whether he could put it all together.

He rose, stretching to his full length, walked inside, and showered. After shaving, he dressed and hurried out, closing the door behind him and leaving George and Van still asleep. Time enough for them later. Right now he needed to see a man.

Casey made his way outside to the street, still damp with the morning dew. The smell of last week's catch of fish mingled with the new, providing an aroma like nothing he'd ever smelled. At least Stateside, he hadn't. A

17

pariah dog slunk by with a carp in his mouth and, on seeing Casey, gave a short, unsure snarl and vanished beneath the porch of a noodle shop. Be careful, dog, he thought, because you're fat enough that I'd give even odds before the week's out you may be gracing the table of some honorable Chinese family.

Casey shivered slightly from the morning chill and dampness. He threaded his way through a maze of indistinguishable residences, shops, and other places he'd rather not think about until finally stopping at the edge of a pier. At the pier's end was the Golden Lotus, one of the town's most expensive restaurants, specializing in the most exquisite cuisine Singapore had to offer. All the delicacies of the east could be found here at the Golden Lotus, and for the true epicure of the exotic, the lowliest and most expensive companions that could be had in the Orient also patronized the place. And drugs! Ling K'ai, the wizened owner of the establishment, had long ago cast his net to the corners of Asia, anywhere that a profit could be found, including that area of Vietnam inhabited by the Kamserai.

Casey knew firsthand of Ling K'ai's dealings with these mercenaries: opium by the hundredweight, opium that had made Ling one of the wealthiest men in the east. Nations might rise and nations might fall, but if a profit were to show, Ling would persevere through all. He would still have contacts there, Casey was sure. Ling personally had no reason to feel fondness for Casey because Romain had cut severely into the man's profits while serving as an adviser to the tribe of the Kamserai, led by one Sou Phang. Sou Phang had become a blood brother to Casey and had curtailed his tribe's opium trade in exchange for CIA gold and guns and the right to rule his people without the interference of the Saigon government.

Phang would conduct raids on the Cambodian side of the border against the Vietcong and the PAVN (Peoples Army of Vietnam) forces, when the Americans and South Vietnamese could not cross over without creating an international incident. He'd often remarked to Casey how stupid it was for the Yankees to provide their enemies a safe refuge to regroup and strike from again. But as long as the Yankees paid well, he was more than glad to do business with them.

If Phang was still in business, Ling would know. He reached the end of the wharf and stopped, taking a deep breath, noticing that the junks were coming in with their morning's catch for the markets and tables of this Oriental Babylon. The small brown waves lapped slowly against the pier's wooden supports again and again, relentlessly, as if to say, "There is no rush; in time you will fall, and the waters will win."

Casey tossed away his second smoke since leaving his room and walked through the open doors. The cleanup coolies were mopping the floors constructed of hand-cut tiles, and Casey knew that each square they cleaned was worth more than they would earn in two weeks of labor. Yet they seemed content with their toil.

He made his way into the cool interior of the Golden Lotus, heading to the rear, where Ling kept his office and living quarters. As he approached the door, a figure detached itself from the shadows and stood in front of him, barring further passage. Casey took in the figure confronting him. Ch'ung Ma, Ling's pet hatchetman and shadow, six and a half feet of twisted muscle that could rip the arm off the average man as a child tears the wings from a butterfly. How many men Ch'ung Ma had sent to their ancestors was a matter of conjecture.

Ch'ung smiled slowly at Casey, proudly displaying a matched set of stainless steel teeth, the kind that the Russians of World War II had been partial to. He looked down at Casey, speaking in sucking sibilants.

"What do you here, long nose? Do you not know that the master has promised you to me when we meet? It is good that you have come to me."

Casey shook his head. "Not now, shit for brains. I want

to see your boss on business. Now get the hell out of my way before I get pissed.''

Ch'ung smiled, light sparkling off his teeth. He bowed and took one step backward. As Casey stepped forward, he straightened and then, leaning back, threw a front snap kick to Casey's throat. Casey moved quickly to the side and deflected the kick with a back knuckle strike to his ankle. Stepping inside, he gave Ch'ung a swinging pointed toe kick in the balls with his right foot. The bodyguard screamed in agony as his testicles were smashed again and again. Casey took a step aside and drop-kicked him in the face three times. Finally the screams subsided, turning into blubbering whimpers.

Ch'ung's condition was illuminated as the door he'd tried to prevent Casey from entering opened suddenly, the interior light now showing the wrecked bloody face of Ling K'ai's favorite toy. Ling's gaze rested first on Casey and then moved to Ch'ung.

"Mr. Romain, am I to be forever disturbed by you? Is he broken?"

Casey looked down at Ch'ung, trying now to pull himself erect with the aid of a chair, his knees still on the floor and his body still wracked by sobbing spasms. Casey moved slightly, aligning himself properly, and delivered a lunging side kick to Ch'ung's spine in the the lower lumbar region. The sound of bone breaking was quite distinct in the dim light of the hallway.

"He is now," Casey replied to Ling's question about his man's condition.

Ch'ung was immobile now. Even the sobbing had ceased. Ling turned to the two coolies who'd stopped their cleaning and had seemingly turned into frozen statues when the trouble started.

"Remove this carrion from my floor. Take it away! I do not wish to see it again."

The two coolies rushed to do their master's bidding, dragging the crippled body of the former troubleshooter out through a side door. Casey heard the muted sound of splashing as they disposed of Ling's trusted and most loyal servant.

Casey turned his eyes to Ling, immaculate in western morning dress as if he were preparing for a breakfast of kippers in England. His age was undeterminable: anywhere from forty-five to sixty-five. Lean, ascetic, his hair thinning slightly and gray on the sides.

"Mr. Romain, why are you here? Surely you know of my feelings toward you, and the fact that you have removed Ch'ung is of no concern to me. It would be a mistake for you to believe that he is my only employee of that caliber. You have exactly one minute to secure my attention, and if you fail to do so, I will have you killed before the next minute enters your life. Now, begin!"

Casey saw additional figures emerge from the shadows, one holding a long-barreled, broom-handled Mauser pistol, a relic from World War I. Ugly but damned effective.

"Major Shan, Mr. Ling. The major sends his regards."

Ling's head jerked slightly at the name. Sucking his breath in back of his teeth, he indicated the door to his office. "Won't you enter and take tea, Mr. Romain?"

"No, Ling! You're not one of my favorite people, either. The only thing I want from you is information for Major Shan, the dashing young officer who castrated your brother with baling wire just to get your attention and cooperation in a small matter you were involved in last year. He allows you to keep your own nuts only because you can occasionally perform a small task for him. If you do this particular service well, it is important enough to him that he may let you off the hook entirely."

Casey grinned, enjoying holding the hammer. "Bring Sou Phang to me in one week, if he still lives. If you lie to me or fail, I can promise you that you'll never have to worry about your sex life again."

Ling shuddered. In his mind he again relived witnessing Major Shan tying the wire around his brother's testicles and ordering two of his men to rip them from the scrotum. The major had been kind enough to allow Ling to shoot his brother and end his suffering. That memory nurtured the fear of the security officer in Ling's mind. The mere mention of Shan's name could produce cold sweats and cause tremors to run throughout his body, as if an attack of malaria had struck him.

Ling K'ai nodded, taking care to control himself. "Phang will be there. Now leave my house and know that the matter between us is not ended. I will have my way with you, and my brother's death would be a blessing compared to what I shall one day do to your filthy white skin. Leave my house! You will be contacted before the week is out."

Casey nodded. There was no need to tell Ling where he lived; the man most likely had known for some time. If he didn't, Casey knew that he would before the next ten minutes had passed. Ling made it a point to know things.

As he left, he thought. Good, if Phang is alive, just maybe I can pull this off.

Ling K'ai turned from Casey and entered his office, closing the door behind him. He went to his desk and sat silently, his head between his hands, trying to get control of himself. He hated Romain. Time and again the man had entered his life, and each time his presence had brought misfortune to Ling. "But enough of these thoughts that torment me," he mumbled. "I will have my day with that swine. For now I must take care of the problem he has posed. Perhaps he is telling the truth; maybe this service I do shall take Shan the butcher's mind and attentions elsewhere and leave me in peace."

He rose and went to a large carved cabinet that Doctor Caligari would have envied. Taking the key from his pocket, he unlocked the doors. Inside was one of the finest shortwave radios that money could buy, with the capability of long-range transmission and the security feature of allowing one to insert and remove the transmission frequency crystals.

Ling checked the instruction notes beside the radio and removed a small box from the drawer beneath it. From the box, he extracted the proper crystal for that day's transmission. Each day a different frequency was used that only he and his agents were aware of.

He turned on the set and waited. Another two minutes until it would be time to transmit. There were several periods set aside each day for all in his service, no matter where they were, to monitor their receivers and see if their call letters had been broadcast. If no signal was received or they had no message to send, they were to wait for five minutes before turning off the set. Each station had a different time in one-hour increments to monitor. If anyone was caught listening to his master's broadcast to another without being previously instructed to do so, there was only one response, and it was exceedingly Chinese in nature and unpleasant in the extreme.

It was time now. Ling pressed the button on his mike and gave the signal letters for his man in charge of the opium trade coming from the triangle in Laos. Part of that trade came through the hands of the bandit Sou Phang, who'd returned to his old occupation as soon as the Americans had left and had quit paying him for other missions more profitable than dope.

Ling spoke to his man in quick, short bursts, letting the half-caste Portuguese-Chinese listen and understand and leaving no doubt as to the seriousness of his orders. Ling instructed him to leave his base of operations on the small island where he now waited, between the new People's Republic of Vietnam and Cambodia, and to find the bandit Sou Phang. He was to return to his island, accompanied by Sou Phang, and Ling would dispatch a small plane from Singapore to pick Phang up within five days.

"Do not fail in this matter," Ling admonished unnecessarily. The half-caste was fully aware of his master's temperament.

Ling signed off and sighed deeply. "It is done; now

back to the business at hand.'' He rose from the cabinet after locking it carefully. ''Perhaps now I should personally inspect the new shipment of girls from Malaya,'' he muttered.

There could possibly be one, he thought, who might be worthy of his attentions before he turned her over to the lesser houses that serviced the sailors and shoremen of Singapore's busy waterfront.

CHAPTER FOUR

Casey took a rickshaw to Padang Park near the town hall. The coolie pulling him moved in a smooth, apparently effortless flow as he weaved in and out of the already crowded traffic of people, automobiles, richshaws, and bicycles. As they headed down Victoria Street, Casey looked over to his left, where Fort Channing lay, and thought of the war memorial fourteen miles from town, where twenty-four thousand servicemen who'd died in World War II were buried. Their remains had been brought here from the battlefields in Malaya and from prisoner of war camps in other occupied countries.

The coolie turned to the right, toward the harbor, and let Casey off between the Victoria Memorial Hall and Theater and the town hall. He walked briskly along the streets, enjoying the sight and smell of the city and its myriad peoples and flavors. A block before the bridge crossing the Singapore River, prior to its reaching the harbor, Casey turned into a shaded alleyway and entered a cool haven from the rising level of human activity on the streets.

The Club New York was a small bistro that offered two things that he'd missed most about the States: refrigerated air conditioning and iced beer.

Casey adjusted his eyes to the dark interior of the dimly lit room and then moved to the bar and ordered a *stengah*, or whiskey and soda, and an ice-cold mug of beer for a chaser.

He used this period of rest to let the events of the morning sink in. Relaxing, he sipped the *stengah* and swallowed the beer. Now that's the way to enjoy beer! The Germans say you taste beer when it's quaffed, a mouthful thrown to the back of the palate, where it's tasted before sliding down with a cool, slightly burning sensation, deep in the throat. "Damn! That's good!"

He checked his watch, a Japanese model; he'd learned to like them in Nam. Exactly eleven-ten, April 4. The Moslems would soon be celebrating Hari Raya Pusa, their festival at the end of Ramadan, where Moslems would neither eat nor drink until sundown. The thought reminded him that he hadn't eaten since the major had laid the problem on his back.

Finishing his *stengah* and quaffing the last of the beer, Casey again ventured out into the increasing heat of the day. Should hit about ninety degrees soon, he thought. Flagging down an old taxi, he had the driver, a nondescript Malayan, take him to the intersection of Cross and Robinson Road. From there he walked to a small restaurant overlooking the Telok Ayer Basin. He seated himself at a table inside with his back against the wall, a habitual gesture, a hangover from the days in Nam and Algeria when it was not uncommon for a grenade to be tossed through the window or open door of a bar or any other place where American soldiers gathered.

Ordering a bowl of chicken and noodles, he lit up a butt and thought of the money. Two hundred thousand! He and the boys would be set for a while. Maybe they'd open a club or hotel outside Kuala Lumpur, or K.L., as the inhabitants had dubbed it, meaning the muddy river mouth. And, he recalled, it damned sure was muddy. Or maybe they would buy a plantation near the Cameroon highlands, where the weather was cool and the hunting was good. A man needs some dreams. Even if he doesn't believe them, he still needs them.

He felt a tug at his insides then, an ache that he had not experienced for some time, as he recalled that one day Van and George would age and pass on and once again he would be alone. *As you are, so shall you be until we . . .* The hell with that shit. He pushed it from his mind. He had them for the time being, and that was more than some men had. Casey finished his food, left a substantial tip for the waiter, and returned to his room near Maxwell Market and the Hindu temple.

He glanced at the knuckles of his right hand. An old scar had opened during contact with Ch'ung's ankle in the scuffle earlier. He grinned. It had already healed and was again scar tissue. Casey entered the room to the sound of Van and George arguing vehemently over who'd drunk the last beer. As he entered, they looked at him and shut up. No words from him were needed; they knew something was in the wind.

"Men, we got a job," Casey laid it out for them afterward, issuing instructions. "Van, you and George get your asses back to K.L. and get our gear together. Also, pay all of our outstanding bills while you're there. I don't want anyone looking for us, especially the Chinese gamblers you owe, Van. Settle everything there and get back here no later than day after tomorrow." He checked his watch. "That'll be the sixth. And Van, keep George the hell away from Mama Chin's girls or he won't be worth a damn for days."

Casey handed Van a thousand from Shan's envelope and grinned. "That ought to be enough to get you home and settle our accounts. When you come back, use Harrison's seaplane. Land near one of the outlying islands and come in from there. Don't forget our special gear, and stay clear of the customs officials, or cops of any kind for that matter. Tell Harrison I'll pay him when he gets here."

Van nodded in understanding and agreement. "No sweat. This refugee from a zoo"—he indicated George—"and myself will be most correct in all matters, my dear boy. Never fear that we shall not prevail over all obstacles, even Mama Chin's darling nieces." Van's father had been an embassy official in London for several years and had sent Van to Eton for two of them. He could speak with an almost uncannily snobbish British accent when he chose, and he chose to often, knowing that it irritated the hell out of Casey.

"Van, just knock off the bullshit and get George the hell out of the john. Both of you get dressed, get fed, and get the hell out of here."

Van laughed, his almond eyes smiling, his boyish face beaming as he hauled George from the bathroom and backed out of the room, bowing to Casey. "Yes, mastah. This boy so happy you honor him with your presence. We now go to do white god's bidding. Thank you, mastah."

Van roared with laughter as he pulled George out of the way of Casey's beer bottle missile and ran down the hall. Before they descended the stairs, George detached himself from Van's tugging arm and pulled himself erect to what he considered to be the majestic height of five foot eight, saying with a great deal of indignation, "Trung Si Casey, you are not a nice man today." With that, he turned and fell down the stairs, accompanied by Van's critique of his diving technique.

Casey smiled to himself as they left. He knew that by the date he'd given them, they would be back with all details taken properly care of.

He felt an affection for these two, a blend of paternalism and brotherhood. The three of them had shared too much together too many times not to love each other in the way that brave and adventurous men do, with respect and laughter.

CHAPTER FIVE

On the day Casey had indicated, a small seaplane set down not twenty miles from where another seaplane, belonging to the Englishman, Harrison, had discharged its cargo of Van, George, and several trunks of special equipment.

But this plane was Ling's, and it carried the key to Casey's entire plan of operation as it taxied in with spray whipping up beside its windows. The man inside wondered why he was being brought here. If it were not that the half-caste had told him that his blood brother waited for him, he would never have left his people.

Things were much too touchy now, with the purges that the Khmer Rouge were inflicting on their own people. Percentage wise, the Khmer Rouge were making Hitler and Stalin look like amateur schoolboys. Already whole areas of the country were empty of life, the fields overgrown and the crops unharvested. He'd heard that one out of every four had been put to death. Men, women, children, even entire families and villages had been wiped out of existence by the liberators of the New Order. "Ah," sighed Sou Phang, "politics is such a danger to the minds of men. It always means someone is going to kill someone else for their own good."

As the plane pulled up to the small wooden pier, Sou Phang rose from his seat. It took him a moment to figure out how the seat belt worked. He'd worn it for the entire trip. These contraptions are not good, he thought. Man should not leave Mother Earth except in the arms of his god or those of his woman when in passion.

The plane came to a halt, and the door was opened immediately. A young Chinese, his face marked heavily by smallpox, motioned for Phang to come ashore and follow him.

"Hurry, old man!" The youngster was evidently impatient.

Phang stretched the muscles in his back and legs from the long period of sitting, walked to the edge of the pier, and dropped his pants. He pissed, joining his yellow stream with the brown waters of the harbor. Giving a sigh of great relief and scratching himself contentedly, he pulled up the bottoms of his Chinese-type pajama suit and turned to the pockmarked lad.

"Be careful how you speak to me, young one, or I may eat your liver before I leave this place."

The young Chinese looked carefully at him, swallowed deeply, and bowed. He'd heard stories of how mean these men were, and more gruesome tales came to mind as he felt his eyes move away from the direct stare of Sou Phang, a chieftain of the Kamserai, one of the last of the free peoples of Indochina.

"Good, young one. You have just taken a step toward knowledge and wisdom. Do not irritate your superiors."

Ling sent a man to Casey's room with the message that Phang had arrived and would be brought to meet him shortly. Ling had further added through the messenger that he desired no more communication with him and prayed that this service would satisfy Major Shan. Casey grinned after hearing Ling's words and told the messenger to leave and to pass on to his master that the feelings were mutual.

Preparing the room for his guest's arrival, beer cooling in a bucket of ice, he laid out the area maps of Cambodia, Vietnam, and Laos neatly on the table. Anticipating his arrival, Van and George were acting like children. Both had a deep liking for the wily chieftain. To Casey, he was a cross between Jesse James and Morgan the pirate.

Time seemed to drag interminably until a voice outside the door announced finally that Sou Phang had arrived.

In a combination of broken English, Vietnamese, and French, Phang yelled from the doorway as to where his welcoming party was and why they had hidden the young women. Casey met him at the door, and it was like stepping into a whirlwind as the chief encircled him with arms like steel, nearly cracking several ribs in the process. Before Casey could catch his breath, Phang was repeating the same act of aggression on George and Van, who were responding in a like manner, each bellowing welcomes between curses and threats against their private parts.

The laughing suddenly ceased as Phang spotted the maps displayed on the table. Silence set in as he leaned over the map showing north to where the Annamite Range entered Cambodia from Laos and Vietnam.

"That is a bad place you have circled there, my son. What can have your interest in that region? There is nothing there for you but death, if you're lucky." He cast his wizened eyes around the room, taking in the equipment that Van and George had brought with them. The folding stock of a Swedish submachine gun extended slightly from beneath the blanket on the bed. That and the expressions on the faces of his three hosts told him that he had struck home with his questions.

Sou Phang sat at the table, exhaled deeply, and spoke. "What is it that you have need of me for, my children?"

Casey explained to him that in the region indicated on the map, a group of Chinese had taken refuge in some caves used previously by Chinese soldiers during the Japanese occupation and that the location of the caves was now known only by the merchant's family, who were assumed to be still safe and unfound. Han's niece's husband, Huan, was one of the band who'd waited and fought from these hills during those desperate years. Now they served again, but Huan was not young. The years and sickness had taken their toll. He had been able to lead the family members there but was unable to take them out and to safety. He'd managed to communicate his location to Han by radio only short minutes before the soldiers of the Khmer Rouge had forced them to flee the small store where they sold and traded with the villagers and hill people. Now they waited. The caves were stocked with food, but it could not last forever. The former Nationalist soldier had been more aware than his employer. He'd seen the signs and had made ready for when the time came. His group consisted of himself, his wife (Han's niece), his eldest daughter, and two small sons, aged four and six.

Phang nodded. "Then what you want to do is get this man and his family out of the caves and return them to their people on Taiwan?"

"That's it," Casey told him. "If you can get me a few of your men to help, I think I know how to do it. Van, George, sit down. This is what I plan. I know only generally the spot where Huan and his family are hiding. You are all familiar enough with that area to know that the foliage is thick enough to hide a complete division in only one square mile. So, Phang, I want you to lend me a few of your best hunters, men who can track and follow spoor and put up a hell of a fight if necessary. I hope it won't come to that. I'm going to try and get in and out without a fight."

Phang nodded his grizzled head. "Yes, I can give you the men. For you I would do it for nothing, but as long as these Chinese thieves are paying, we might as well make a small profit, no?"

Casey grinned, nodding. "No argument from me, old friend. What do you want?"

"Twenty ounces of gold for each man. An additional twenty for each one killed or wounded to a degree that he can no longer do his work. Is that agreeable?"

"Agreed," said Casey.

"Five men for one hundred ounces of gold, paid in advance?" the old man queried.

"As you say, friend Phang." Casey smiled. "How are you fixed for ammo and weapons?"

The old one shrugged. "We have most of what you left for us and some we picked up here and there. If there is any specialty you may require, you'll have to bring it along."

"No problem." Casey turned to Van. "Go to the airport and wait for Shan. He'll be arriving in about an hour. No stops along the way, Van. Get him here as fast as you can."

His friend nodded in understanding. There was no time for jokes or facetiousness now. There was work to be done. While Van might play the fool now and then, it was merely for his own entertainment. In a fight, he was one of the most efficient killing machines Casey had ever seen. With the expert swinging of George's native short sword, they were a pair to give any man nightmares.

Van departed, leaving George to watch the door of the room so that he could keep the curious away. They knew Ling was around, and far from uninterested in their project. His men would be watching their every move, taking notes on all they witnessed, even raiding their garbage for telltale signs of their plans. Casey was wise to their gambits, and the room was never left vacant. They did their own cleaning and checked the trash carefully before setting it out.

Casey and his guest, Phang, waited. They talked quietly of the pros and cons of different aspects of the upcoming mission. Time passed rapidly, and two raps at the door told them that Van had arrived with the major.

Shan entered the room, taking in everything and everyone inside. He gave a short bow as he turned to Phang. "May the gods give you a long life and peace," he said.

Phang rose and bowed in return. "It is truly an honor to be in the presence of such a great soldier."

Both men, satisfied that courtesy had been observed, sat down and waited for Casey to make the next move. When he hesitated, the major spoke.

"You have a plan, Mr. Romain?"

Casey stood and walked to a chair opposite the major. Sitting down, he pointed to an area of the map. "The village of Sien Dap, that's the area, Major. Twenty kilometers due north of the town is a field of elephant grass. We went through it once, Phang and me, on a recon mission several years ago. It's a very short distance from there to the family in the caves. This is the only drop zone I can think of in that area that could be considered safe, mainly because there's no damned reason for anyone to be there. It's neither commercial nor strategic."

Shan frowned. "Did you say drop zone, Mr. Romain?"

"Yes, we're going to parachute in, Shan. You said you could provide aircraft, and by God, that's what I want. What type doesn't matter as long as it get us and about three hundred pounds of supplies in there safely."

The major thought it over. "Yes, we in security do occasionally send a flight over occupied countries. There actually isn't much risk involved, as the reds are very short on radar equipment. Their planes stay close to home base and make few flights, since their fuel supply is short. But you must give me warning enough so that I may check the weather conditions in advance. That could be the only thing that could delay your flight. Otherwise, there should be no difficulty getting you safely into your target area."

Casey nodded. "Good. We'll also need three chutes and drop bags for our gear. Get the modified Tojo chutes if you can, Major. We'll be jumping at night, and I like having a steerable chute in case we're off center a bit. Avoiding trees or dangerous objects is a lot easier with the Tojo."

The major agreed again. Everything would be as Romain had requested. Now, one question if he might. "Let us assume you are in safely. How do you plan on getting them out?"

Casey laughed. "With the aid of two more of your planes, Major. We're going to do a skyhook."

"Skyhook?" responded Shan quizzically. "Skyhook? None of my people have ever been involved in that kind of lift before."

Casey shook his head. "We've got to have them. If things should go down the wrong way, Huan's youngsters would never survive a trip through the jungle. If we're going to get them out, it's got to be this way. Check your air force, Major. There must be some people there who were trained at Fort Bragg in the art of skyhooking. One damned thing's for sure; the distance is too great for a chopper to reach, and there's no place for a plane to set down. It has to be this way, so request that the equipment and harnesses be shipped over as soon as possible. Rest assured, Major, that we don't move without them."

Shan nodded in agreement. The garden seemed a lot farther off now than before, but it was still within sight.

"Very well, Mr. Romain. I will get the men, the planes, and the necessary equipment. What is your time schedule?"

Casey turned to Phang. "How long will it take you to get your men to this field by Sien Dap?"

Phang thought it over carefully, studying the map again and mentally going over the trip in his mind. "Ten days from the time I return to my village. If we go by sampan a good distance up the Mekong and then cut across country, we will be there in ten days."

Casey turned to Shan. "Did you bring the items I requested?"

Shan nodded. "I left them outside with your man, the savage."

"He's not my man, Major, he is my friend."

Going to the door, he called for George to come in. He took the case from him and laid it on the table before opening it. Inside was a modified single sideband radio, not much larger than a cassette tape recorder, but Japanese technology had made it the latest and most efficient available for long-distance transmitting and receiving. He checked its batteries and turned to Phang.

"Take this and return to your people, old friend. Each night when the sun sets, turn it on and wait for a signal for one hour. If within that time period you don't receive, try again each night until you do. That will be your signal to leave for the field outside Sien Dap. Start listening to the radio on the evening of one week from today. Go now with the major, and he will arrange the payment we agreed on. I informed him earlier, when I knew you were coming, of your preference for gold. He has arranged for the funds to be available here, so get your money and return this night to your people. I fear we may run short of time." Casey put his arms around the old man and hugged him. "Farewell, old friend."

Shan rose and started to leave with Phang to complete their transaction. Before reaching the door, he turned to Casey. "I too will be leaving. I have no time to spare, either. I will get all that you require, Mr. Romain. Farewell, and may the gods be with you in our mutual mission."

After they'd left, Casey called George in and poured them each a long pull from the cherished remains of a bottle of Tennessee sipping sour mash. Raising his glass high in a toast, he grinned. "Well, you old warthog, it looks like everything is go."

George drank and made a face. Casey looked at him. "What the hell's the matter, you miserable barbarian? Don't you know how hard it is to get good whiskey?"

George grunted, replying that he much preferred Malayan whiskey. It had more flavor.

"More flavor? You silly shit, that's formaldehyde that you've been tasting in that rat poison you call whiskey."

George smiled. "Trung Si"—his Vietnamese term for "sergeant"—"it is a shame that you've never learned to appreciate the good things of the Orient. But obviously, you will never have any taste at all."

Casey roared at him. "No taste? You dog-eating molester of water buffalo. Did you say no taste?"

George nodded, his eyes shining. "See, you even have no appreciation for a nice young roasted puppy. So sad, Trung Si, so sad. You miss many good things."

Both men fell into spasms of laughter that could be easily heard by the locals for at least a city block.

CHAPTER SIX

Phang, after being paid, was on his way back to his village. Ling's plane was flying low to avoid radar and making its way without lights across the island. It then vectored for the half-caste's island.

Major Shan landed at Taiwan Airport just as the rosy glow of dawn broke, showing that day was not far behind. Not stopping to go home, he went instead directly to his office at the base, carefully closing the door behind him.

Shan began immediately to put his plans into operation. He was an example of extreme efficiency. Making maximum use of his position in the security section and the phones at his disposal, he began making the necessary calls, threatening some and bribing those he could not threaten.

He arranged for the next group of exchange students studying in the States to bring back with them the equipment that Casey had said would be necessary for a skyhook operation. Helium and balloons, harnesses and winch, lines, and the strange V-shaped device that was mounted on the nose of the pickup aircraft. Enough for six. He'd had no trouble with these arrangements. The Americans, as usual, were more than happy to show off their equipment and how well it worked. A call to a senator acquaintance on the Defense Appropriations Committee hadn't hurt, either. Everything required was on its way to him within three days. For thirty-six hours, Shan had whipped himself into a work frenzy. All that could be done was done. Now to wait. Two days until all would be delivered, leaving some leeway in case the weather turned bad. Time to contact Romain and his beasts. Time for them to come to Taiwan for final preparations.

Shan made the call to Casey and arranged for a small plane to bring the soldiers of fortune from Singapore to Taiwan. In this manner, their movements would be covered, and the plane crew were all members of Shan's staff. They would be silent. After all, their commander was involved in security, and if he was to bring these men to the base, he must have a reason.

Information came in many forms, including a flight line mechanic, one Wu Lee Tsu. Wu was a fine mechanic but suffered from the common disease known as greed. He occasionally, in order to supplement the small pay that the Nationalist Air Force allowed him, hid packets of narcotics on board planes heading for many destinations. For this small service, a businessman in Singapore would deposit to his personal account five hundred Hong Kong dollars for each and every cache he put aboard. Wu had been told to keep alert for anything involving Major Shan and some foreigners, especially one known as Romain. The mechanic had earned a nice bonus when he'd informed his mentor in Singapore about the arrival in Taiwan of three disreputable-looking men, including a round-eye named Casey Romain. The mechanic's report made its way to the ears of one Ling K'ai, of the former crown colony of Singapore. Ling sent orders for the mechanic to be on the alert for additional information as to the movements and activities of the foreign group, especially their destination when and if they departed Taiwan.

Wu sensed that something out of the ordinary was in the wind. The tone of Ling's orders spelled money if he played his cards right. Asking temporary leave of absence from his position, he became a shadow to the three strange men. The mechanic was outside the merchant Han's home when Casey, his two friends, and Major Shan were inside for the final stages of their planning.

Inside, Casey had the floor, explaining to Han what a skyhook was and his plan for its use. Short and to the point, he told the merchant how an adult or child could be put into a special harness, connected to a line attached to a helium-filled balloon. When released, it would rise to an altitude of two to three hundred feet. Then a specially equipped aircraft would fly into the line, just below the balloon, capturing the line and throwing it up against the rear of the plane. The crew would then attach special hoists to the line and reel in the strapped-in cargo of terrified humanity. Casey agreed with Han. Yes, it did look dangerous. But in reality, very few accidents had come from the use of this procedure.

Casey told them of the time he'd watched the commanding general of the Special Warfare Center at Fort Bragg, North Carolina, being lifted out of the training and demonstration area, named after a Sergeant Gabriel, with this procedure. And if the American brass could do it, it had to be safe enough for kids.

The merchant Han looked askance at Major Shan. Shan replied that he too had seen this operation while training in the States, and while it looked dangerous, he'd never seen anyone hurt while performing it.

Han asked, "How do they prevent the one being lifted in this manner from being smashed into trees or other obstacles as he is being lifted into the air by this plane? Surely one must be carried forward for a long distance before one begins to rise. The forward motion of the plane would ensure that, no?"

It was Casey who answered. "No, merchant Han. That is not true. I agree that it seems that way, but with all the factors working, when the plane snags the line, it is traveling so fast that the harness's cargo is immediately lifted over thirty meters straight up before it begins a forward motion. A man can be lifted from an area less than ten feet in diameter with this method."

Han nodded. ''I still do not quite comprehend, but I shall leave the matter in your hands. You are the experts; I am but a poor dealer in goods. But take care my family is not harmed.''

The evening closed with Han arranging for his banker to transfer one hundred thousand American dollars to the account of Casey Romain of Kuala Lumpur in Malaya.

''This being resolved, when will you leave, Mr. Romain?''

Outside the window, Wu listened eagerly for the long nose's response. This information could bring him big money.

''We will leave as soon as we've made certain that our people in Cambodia are in position and ready. The major says our equipment is due in at any time, and we'll have to check it all out carefully during our wait. I would estimate that all would be ready within twelve to fourteen days. We will time our arrival over the drop zone so as to arrive early in the morning just before dawn. Sien Dap will be asleep, and the farmers will be inside with their wives.''

Han nodded. ''That is good. And when will you attempt to have the members of my family lifted in this most extraordinary manner from the jungle and returned to me?''

Casey thought for a moment before answering. ''We don't know the exact position of your people, so it may take us a day or two to locate them.'' He turned to Shan. ''Give me three days after the drop, and at midnight on the third day, send the plane over, and for three nights thereafter at the same hour if no signal is received on the first. If he receives our signal by the fourth night, he will drop the lift harnesses and supplies to us and circle until he spots the first balloon, then reel us in one by one.''

He turned to Han. ''If there is no signal by the fourth night, you will have saved one hundred thousand dollars and lost a family.''

Wu, the mechanic outside the window, began to tremble in nervous anticipation of the reward he would receive for this information. Silently, he faded back across the wall through the shadows of the garden. One small leap, and he was up and over, his passage unnoticed by anyone.

Wu went directly to the contact of Ling, giving him the information he'd received and adding afterward that the information should be worth at least five thousand American dollars to the honorable Ling K'ai. This amount, he knew, would be enough to set him free and allow him to start his own business in Hong Kong or even Kowloon. These were his needs.

The contact looked at him, smiling slowly at the fool's demands. Did not the foolish mechanic know of Ling's temperament? Standing directly before Wu, with no hesitation, he delivered a hooking blow to the smaller man's solar plexus. Wu collapsed, a surprised look flashing over his face, just before the pain took over.

Shan drove Casey and his men to a safe house mounted in the foothills near the base and placed them on a twenty-four-hour security alert around its perimeter. The only phone was a direct line to his office. They could venture outside only to the walled garden, and no visitors were allowed. He would gamble nothing at this point. The garden of the merchant Han was almost close enough to touch.

Early the following morning in his office, a routine message was passed on to Shan that an aircraft mechanic employed at the base had been found dead outside a notorious house of gambling and prostitution. The only thing out of the ordinary, it seemed, was the look of extreme agony on the man's face. The only visible mark on the body was a small bruise on the chest. The major thought about it for a moment and shrugged it off. He had no time to concern himself with a peasant aircraft mechanic.

At the same time, in Singapore, a courier from the contact in Taipei was delivering Wu's information to Ling K'ai. He was pleased to find that it came free of charge.

At the safe house, Casey had cut off the booze. They all needed time to dry out and prepare for the mission that lay ahead. In their condition, and with the laxity of the past months, it was actually not enough time. But he and the boys were still in pretty good shape, he supposed.

The time passed slowly, almost creeping. In the house of Lin Pao Lieh, the old man sat, thinking of the things his nephew had told him late last night, of these strange men and their methods, odd and discomforting methods that he did not fully understand. Lin Pao soothed his mind by letting the fingers of his right hand run over the smoothness of the bronze Chueh wine goblet he held, caressing the three knifelike legs, taking comfort from the centuries it had endured. Thirteenth century B.C., he remembered. Shang Yin dynasty, old with the patina of ages yet sound and waiting serenely for the next three thousand years to pass. We must be as this goblet. We the people of the old country. We must ever wait for each cycle to be completed in its own time. If the old man had known the man called Casey Romain, one who'd heard and learned of this philosophy many years before, he would have known a man in complete agreement. Lin's thought process continued. Nothing we say or do can ever change but little the gods' timetables for our lives and histories.

The feel of the cool bronze beneath his aged and wrinkled hands gave him comfort, and, slowly rocking back and forth as children and old men will do, he dreamed of centuries gone, of empires risen and fallen. For the old man, this dream never ended, and almost without knowning it, he joined his memories.

Late in the afternoon of the same day, Shan received word that the equipment from America had arrived at the airport on base. Picking up the direct line to the safe house, he called Casey. The phone rang twice before George picked it up, mumbling something unintelligible in his native dialect. Shan swore at him in English, and George laughed.

"I didn't know that you spoke Bihar, Chinaman."

Shan retorted, "I don't, you dog!"

George chuckled and replied. "Then how could you repeat exactly what I said to you, Major?"

Major Shan turned livid with rage.

"Wait one minute, Major. Here is Trung Si Casey now." After handing the phone to Casey, George fell over laughing.

Casey could still hear Shan cursing over the phone. He held the receiver away from his ear and yelled in to the mouthpiece. "Stop yelling, Major. It's me, Romain."

Major Shan's voice toned down to a muted choking. "Mr. Romain, I have had about all I can endure of you and your men's vulgar behavior. This is your last warning. Contract or no contract, if you or one of your beasts gives me any more trouble, you will not have to worry about getting into Cambodia, for you will never leave Taiwan. Do I make myself clear to you, absolutely clear? Mr. Romain, do you understand me?"

He was almost screaming now, and his raving reminded Casey of Li Tsao's adamant rage and yelling, when she'd tried to offer her body for his secret of life. When he'd refused, she'd screamed at him in rage and had had him buried alive. It was a page in his life that he'd tried desperately to forget. He had a great fear of tight places. What was it the Americans called it? Claustrophobia? That had been one hell of an experience.

Casey took a deep breath and got back to the business at hand. Boy, was the major pissed off! He adopted a conciliatory tone in his reply to the major's tirade.

"Take it easy, Major. You know George is too dumb to mean anything derogatory. He's just a poor ignorant savage."

Shan quieted down. "Perhaps," he said, "what you say is true. But what I have just told you is also true. Do not try my patience any further, either of you." The flat tone of Shan's voice told Casey that the man was not fooling around. It would be best to cool it.

"Okay, Major, no more games. All business now. What do you want?"

"Your equipment has arrived, Mr. Romain. It shall be delivered to your location this evening. As soon as I hang up the phone, I will dispatch the signal plane toward Sou Phang's headquarters. When they are within his range, they will transmit the signal to warn him of the departure. It would appear to me, Mr. Romain, that you and your . . . whatever they are can plan on being in the air and out of my sight within ten days' time. I do not have to tell you the results if you fail in this mission, do I? The Khmer Rouge are exceedingly unpleasant to unexpected guests.''

"Very good," replied Casey. "I read you five by five. No mistakes, and no ties whether win or lose. Anything else, Major?"

"No, Mr. Romain, that is all. Good night."

Casey hung up his end of the phone and turned to Van and George. "Gentlemen, it's a definite go. The equipment has arrived from the States and will be here shortly. We crap out early tonight and get an early start tomorrow."

George and Van offered no comment. Without anything being added, they knew the party was over. From here on out, the name of the game was professionalism.

CHAPTER SEVEN

Dawn rose gray and foggy, with a light mist chilling the air. Casey roused his men. A light breakfast of rice and boiled duck eggs started their day, along with coffee and tea: good Chinese tea so hot that it almost scalded the mouth if one was not careful.

Chow finished, each man went to his room and took out his own equipment. Casey's instructions upon the arrival of Shan's cargo from the States had been to check their individual gear prior to checking the skyhook rigs.

Van opened a custom-made case and removed a German-made G-3 assault rifle, 7.62 Nato, semi or fully automatic. It was capable of four hundred fifty rounds per minute and extremely accurate for a military weapon, firing from a closed bolt. It was an extrapolation of the World War II German MP 44-45 assault rifle, the *sturm gehwer*. A small attaché case held not only the telescopic sight for the piece but also a special attachment that had cost dearly, a silencer stolen from the Spanish secret police, who also used this rifle but manufactured it as the *Cetme*. Van had bought the weapon last year from a defecting Spanish agent who held no love for the current regime and needed some travel money. Casey had schooled him well in its use. Van was still puzzled at Casey's knowledge of weapons of German origin. Where had the man learned so much?

In the adjoining room, George was busily cleaning his own piece, a Savage automatic shotgun, the type used by most prison guards in the United States, Casey had informed him. But this one had a perforated cooling jacket around the barrel and a bayonet attachment. George had become fond of this type of weapon while serving with the Special Forces up in II Corps. The effect that the 12-gauge double 00 buckshot had on the human body was amazing. Coupled with the special twenty-round magazines Casey had made for him, it gave the weapon a personality of its own. You could hit an elephant in the ass with it and knock his brains out. This piece, and the modified machete, or short sword, depending on how you looked at it, made this small, wiry combination of sinew and cartilage as deadly as a tree cobra.

Casey Romain laid out his gear carefully, separating each piece, examining it in turn, and setting it aside: a Swedish "K" submachine gun, 9-mm caliber, ten magazines of ammo, an additional two hundred fifty rounds in boxes, one bayonet, and a survival kit. Rations consisted of dehydrated chow and soups. These, along with a small sack of rice, would last a week and weighed no more than three pounds. Two collapsible canteens, each with a two-quart capacity, for one got very thirsty in the jungle. Changes of socks, since a man's feet could start to rot in three days if he wore the same pair without changing. Boots, the canvas-sided GI jungle boots from Nam with the steel plates removed from the soles. They gave him blisters, and besides, he didn't think there'd be a problem with mines or *punji* stakes at this late date.

Casey took out his pride and joy from the final box: a WWII Kraut MG-34 light machine gun, lightweight and with a cyclic rate of fire as yet unmatched as far as he was concerned. It could fire from both belt and a side-mounted drum. A beautiful gun—no wasted metal and as accurate as anything ever produced. He would carry this one on the mission. It had been rechambered to the ammo of the NATO 7.62; that way, Van's ammo and his machine gun

would be as one. The LMG and the box of rifle grenades
were his heavy armaments. He recalled his first introduc-
tion to the piece he was holding, or at least one identical
to it. His name had been Langers then, and it had been
four decades ago. Instead of Van and George, his comrades in arms had been called Teacher and Gus. Damn, he
still missed them at times. He could still see Teacher's
face in his memory now: the waxy paleness, the trembling
of his hands as he had unslung the Schmiesser and said
good-bye to Langers, staying behind as he desired and
throwing his life into the destruction of the hated SS
killers. And Gus? He'd disappeared in a village near Jo-
hannesburg during a hellish barrage of Russian artillery.
Gus Beidemann. He looked more like a panther than a
man, could fart on command, and could drink Russian
vodka faster than the bastards could distill it. It had been
good to find him still alive and kicking at the training
camp in Sidi Slimane, serving with others of the Reich
who had taken refuge in the legion. Only once more after
the legion had they fought together on a private mission,
but even that seemed a long time ago. He placed the
memory back where it belonged and returned the LMG to
its container.

Shortly before noon that day, each man had finished
going over his gear. Everything had been checked out,
cleaned, and put in readiness. Lives had been lost, they
were all aware, because of broken shoelaces. Nothing
could be left to chance.

Van and George entered Casey's room when he called.
Smiling, he gave each a supply of quarter-grain syrettes of
morphine. "Don't use these unless absolutely necessary,
or I may have to get more from our favorite dope pusher,
Mr. Ling."

Van grinned slyly. "Trung Si, when this one is over,
and before we retire, if we do, you do know that one of us
is going to have to kill Ling K'ai, don't you?"

Casey nodded as Van continued. "I would consider it a
great honor and a personal favor if you would allow me

the pleasure of terminating the existence of that piece of filth.''

Casey looked closely at his friend. ''I know you're right, Van, but I had planned on snuffing him myself. But why should I have all the fun? Okay, he's yours when we get back, under one condition. You take George along, and you try nothing tricky. You just take him out. The bastard is smart, and if you should miss, he'll be on our asses like ugly on an ape. So don't screw with him. Is all your gear checked out?'' He looked from one to the other, and they both nodded. ''Good! Let's take it easy for the rest of the day; then we'll start checking the pickup equipment in the morning. It's too damned hot out in the garden to do it this afternoon. We'll have to spread the balloons out and check them for leaks, the pressure on the helium, and all that crap. We got our work cut out for us while Phang moves his men up the Mekong. Now, out of my room, you heathens. I got me some sleeping to catch up on.''

They returned to their rooms. Casey lay on his bed, staring at the ceiling.

Premission butterflies and excited anticipation kept him awake.

Well, this was the big one. No more shoot 'em ups for a while after this one. He was going to lie in the sun and stuff his carcass with baked baby pig, roasted bananas, and toddies. Lots and lots of toddies. But it wouldn't last long, he knew. The urge for action would strike again. War and fighting were too deeply instilled in him, and inactivity was not one of his strong points. He was a doer, a gladiator, a soldier. Finally, he fell into a light and troubled sleep, fighting over again the battles and places he wished he could forget. The arenas of Rome, the white snow-covered fields of Russia, the heavy dampness of the jungles in Nam, Hitler's bunker and the odor of cyanide. Throughout the dreams, as if superimposed cinematically, the sad face of the Jew, Jesus, supervising all scenes.

Watching . . . waiting . . . *For as you are, so shall you remain until we meet again.* The great circle . . . circle . . . circle. Was there no end for the soldier Casca Rufio Longinus? Was what lay ahead to be identical to the past? He tossed fitfully in his sleep.

The following morning, after a quick breakfast, they commenced a thorough checking of their skyhook equipment. Other than storage fatigue, it all was in perfect order. All was ready now, and the following days of waiting passed, seeming to creep now, as sunrise turned to sunset and his friend, Phang, with his hunters, moved just as slowly up the Mekong, making their way to the designated point of rendezvous. They waited. Impatient but determined, they waited.

Early on the afternoon of the eleventh day, Casey again lay tossing in haunted sleep. He was now in a Caribou aircraft waiting to make a jump. The tailgate was down, and the trooper was counting off. One, okay. Two, okay. Stand in the door! The warning bell sounded. Casey opened his eyes, lost for a moment, and then reached for the phone that had pulled him away from his dream.

"Hello! Yes. All right. In ten minutes. Right, we'll be ready." Hanging up the phone he called, "Van, George, we leave in ten minutes for the hangar. Get your shit together."

Right on the button, an American deuce and a half truck pulled up in front of the safe house and blew its horn once. Casey and his men began moving their gear outside and loading it aboard the truck. The driver offered no help. If he had, it would have been refused. At this point, no one would be allowed to touch their equipment but themselves.

When all was loaded, the three men jumped inside and seated themselves against the canvas siding; the hard wooden slats made their presence known. The driver dropped the tarp in the rear, leaving them in shadowed darkness, with bright flashes of light breaking through now and then in the openings of the canvas.

The driver slowed at the entrance of Taiwan Airbase, flashed his ID and was admitted without search. Shan had done his job well. As they passed, the guard had already moved to the phone, calling security to relay the message that the truck had arrived.

Shan's office was closer to the designated hangar, and he arrived before the truck. He swung the doors open wide just as the vehicle pulled in. He motioned them inside the hangar, closing the double doors immediately behind himself. The driver jumped down quickly, slinging his M-16, and moved to the front of the hangar, mounting guard.

Casey and his men jumped from the rear of the truck, their eyes adjusting slowly to the well-lit interior. Shan turned to Casey, his voice sharp and authoritative.

"You will remain here until departure. Leave your equipment on the truck until it is time to move it to the plane. Word has been received that Phang is in position and ready. I will be leaving you now; there is much for me to do. I will return one hour before departure time. There is food and drink over there by the workbenches. Do not, I repeat, do not venture outside this building. It is at your own peril if you do so."

With that cheerful note, Shan walked away, returning to his office across the flight line, having to slow before crossing while a C-130 landed.

Inside the hangar, the metal roof magnified the outside heat of midafternoon. The first to remove his shirt was Casey. Then, as the sweat flowed, the other two followed suit. The sight of Casey's upper torso—the scars that were too many to count, one so deep that no one could hold doubt that it had been meant to be fatal—never ceased to hold Van and George in awe. He appeared to them as if he'd been standing in the direct path of a 155-mm round when it had gone off and had caught every piece of shrapnel it had contained.

They moved to the workbench and made sandwiches,

the heat forcing them to chase the food with salt tablets. Casey raised his paper cup of water in toast.

"No beer, no whiskey, and no toddies for the bodies, boys, until we get back. Let's hope this one is an easy one. Kompai! Kompai, you bandits!"

After eating, they changed into jungle camouflage, adjusting their webbing, and filled one canteen each. Again they waited.

Van and George lay amid a pile of parachutes when Shan entered the hangar. Casey studied the maps.

"It is time, Mr. Romain. Is all in order?"

Casey nodded as the major pointed and spoke again. "Unload the pickup equipment in that corner. It will not be touched until time to bring it in to your drop zone." He turned to walk off. "Come with me, Romain."

Casey followed, grinning and noticing that the major had dropped the "mister." Van and George loaded the chutes and drop bags back aboard the truck.

"Look, Major, I know you don't care much for us, but we've always done you a good job in the past, and this time will be no different. Like we agreed before, it's all business, no games. After this one, though, it's quits for us. Agreed?"

Shan quickly agreed, seeing no reason not to. After all, he was the one in control and could do what he wished later.

"Agreed, Mr. Romain. When this is over, we go our separate ways. Now get your men on the truck. We've no time to waste."

The guard, after a motion of Shan's hand, opened the doors wide and returned to his truck. Assuring himself that the men were loaded, he pulled out of the hangar, with Shan's sedan bringing up the rear. With the lights on dim, they traversed the runway to the far end of the field. It was dark now, the area lit only by the runway landing lights. Flames were shooting out of the cowlings of the old C-119, which was now warming up and waiting for the three passengers. The tailgate was dropped, inviting the comment of George as they climbed out of the truck how much it reminded him of a female water buffalo from the rear. Ready to be mounted.

They wasted no time transferring their gear to the waiting plane, heeding the cargo master's instructions as to where he wanted it stowed. Van and George were fastening their seat belts as Shan turned to Casey outside the plane.

Shouting to be heard over the frantic roar and blast of the aircraft's props, Major Shan spoke.

"Everything is done, Mr. Romain. Have a safe journey. Perform your task well, and we shall both be wealthy men."

Casey smiled. Shan had finally admitted that he too was turning a good buck from this venture.

"The pickup aircraft, I assure you, will be at your drop zone on schedule and waiting for your signal to drop the skyhook gear. From here on, it is all in your hands. Good luck, Mr. Romain." Again he didn't offer his hand.

Casey nodded and entered the plane. The tailgate closed. The interior of the C-119 was lit only by a single red light that cast an eerie glow over the faces of those inside. The cargo master, a tough-looking little man, motioned for Casey to find a spot and sit down. Over the entrance to the cockpit, the "No Smoking" light blinked in English and Chinese. The throbbing roar of the engine nestled around them as the plane gave a series of small jerks that told them it was beginning to turn and head for the apron in preparation for takeoff. The old bird taxied a short distance and settled down momentarily, with the pilot waiting for clearance. When he got the word, he gave the gas to the air relic and locked her brakes. Throbbing and shaking, she settled back like a sentry dog getting ready to leap. He released the brakes then, and the aged machine lunged forward, lurching, gaining speed, wheels humming along the asphalt and concrete runway past the lights of the control tower. Suddenly she was up. The throbbing eased somewhat, not loud or severe now without the ground to reverberate from. The buoyancy felt good to Casey. This was the real him—action, doing. This was his life.

The C-119 continued climbing until the designated altitude was reached. The pilot checked his magnet, and they left the flight path, heading out over the straits between their present position and the lesser islands of Quemoy.

One stop at Clark Air Force Base in the Philippines, for fuel, and they'd move on to their target area. Casey told the men that it was okay to unfasten their seatbelts. They did so, and both moved immediately to their chutes, reclined, and went to sleep.

Good idea, he thought. I'll try that myself after I smoke this butt and think a bit. Best not to think too much, though. Ah, piss on it! I smoke too much anyway. He put the unlit cigarette back in the pack and joined his men.

Relaxing as best he could on the small canvas seats that ran along the side of the plane, Casey closed his eyes, listening to the engines. His head bounced as they hit some turbulence, snapping his eyes back open for a second. Then they closed again.

This was all very familiar, a plane carrying him to a place where men in their right mind would never think of going. The first time he had gone in a C-119, it was known as French Indochina and covered all of Vietnam, Laos, and Cambodia. Now he was going back. It seemed he was always going back somewhere.

He shifted his butt over to ease the growing numbness in it and sighed deeply, letting the air out slowly. He was letting his mind go back into the hellhole of Dien Bien Phu.

He would always have a bitter taste in his mouth about that—too many good men lost for no purpose. (*Le legion, le legion, enevant le legion.*) It all came to him riding on the hum of the engines. He had been with the BEP, the 1er Batallion étranger de parachutistes, brought in with the 8e

Parachutistes de Choc (8 BPC) to add their strength to the other legion battalions, the 1st and 3rd of the 13e Demi-Brigade and the 2e regiment étranger, all containing strong German contingents. The legion had been the only refuge for many of them after the fall of Germany, and the French needed professional soldiers to rebuild their empire.

He had enlisted while Berlin was still smoldering and had taken the name Casey Romain, as it was time to put Carl Langers behind him. The enlistment officer for the Étrange didn't care what name you signed up under as long as you knew how to fight, and once he had a close look at his new volunteer, there had been no doubt about his capabilities. The new name would also apply to the new citizenship papers he would receive when he had finished his enlistment, and papers were vital.

When they hit the ground, he knew they were in trouble. One look at the mountains around them and only one road by which to bring supplies, lying where it would be no problem to be cut off either by ambush or shell fire. He began to wish that he had deserted while still in Algeria.

It didn't take long for the shit to start, and for the next fifty-five days, he'd never know a full night's sleep.

There were five major strong points around Dien Bien Phu—Anne-Marie, Claudine, Dominique, Eliane, and Hugunette. Two hundred yards north of Anne-Marie stood an isolated strong point on a small height, Gabrielle, and one-thousand five-hundred yards north-east of Dominique on the northern approach of Rd. 41 stood Beatrice. Six thousand yards south of Claudine, protecting the airstrip and southern approaches, was Isabelle. Isabelle, a pretty name for a place where so much dying would occur. It was there that he stayed for most of his time, leaving the barbed wire surrounding their bunkers only for brief spoiling patrols or to reopen the road to Dien Bien Phu when the Viets cut it, which occurred frequently.

Casey had been in enough battles to know that the place was a trap. Dien Bien Phu's position covered an area eleven miles long and three wide, on ground that had been stripped. They'd had to tear down the native villages for lumber to cover their shelters and to shore up the sides of the bunker walls. On either side of them rose jagged hills two thousand feet higher than Dien Bien Phu's position. There was no way to prevent the Vietminh from taking up placements on them and setting artillery where it could fire down the throats of the defenders, even though Colonel Piroth, who commanded the artillery at Dien Bien Phu had made the boast that the Vietminh wouldn't get their artillery through to here. If they did get there, the colonel would smash them. Even if they managed to keep on shooting, they would be unable to supply their pieces with enough ammunition to do any real harm. He based his faith in the general staff's belief that the Vietminh was not capable of bringing up enough guns to do any damage. It was just too difficult an operation in this kind of terrain, and partly on the strength of his own force, which consisted of two groups, with twelve 105 howitzers each and a strong battery of four 155-mm guns with more range and power than anything the Vietminh were known to possess. All this, along with three heavy mortar companies and four quad fifties, those deadly four-barreled 50-caliber heavy machine guns.

Casey knew Piroth was wrong from the start. He had long known the Asian capability for doing things the Occidental mind thought impossible. The Vietminh broke down their artillery into pieces and hand carried them through the jungle, hacking their way up to the top of the ridges, a back-breaking job that no modern Western general would have dared to ask his men to attempt. The Vietminh didn't question Giap's orders, and they hauled up forty-eight 105s of the same type as the French, which came in handy later, when air drops missed Dien Bien Phu and landed in Vietminh lines, supplying them with several days' worth of ammunition. Along with the 105s were forty-eight 75-mms, forty-eight 120-mm mortars, many 75-mm recoilless rifles, and around forty heavy antiaircraft guns. With these, the Viets controlled access to and from the valley.

On March 13, Giap gave his orders, and the first salvos began to fall on the outlying strong points to the north of the airstrip; Anne-Marie, Beatrice, and Gabrielle. After them the airfield was pounded, cratering the runway to make it nearly impossible to land a plane safely and to destroy most of the Bearcat fighters on the ground. Which they did! Only three out of eleven managed to get airborne; the rest burned on the runway.

This was the beginning of the end. For a week, the Vietminh pounded everything in the valley. Soon, Death Volunteers began to hurl themselves at the wire surrounding the fortifications. Hurling their bodies onto the wire, they would set off explosives taped to themselves in an attempt to blast open a path through which their comrades could attack.

Beatrice was targeted for special attention and saturated by mind- and will-breaking heavy fire and constant ground assaults. It was manned by a unit Casey knew well, the 3/13 Demi-Brigade, de l'étrange, a wholly European force of seven hundred fifty-nine tough veterans from every side of World War II who now fought side by side against the common enemy.

Suicide squads blasted openings in the defenses and infantry poured through as the Viet guns zeroed in on the French artillery batteries in the center of the camp, knocking out two of the 105s and killing most of their Senegalese crews, taking out the command bunker and wiping out the commander of Beatrice and his staff in one burst of flame and smoke. The three companies remaining were left to fight on their own. By nine-thirty, two of them had gone off the air. The third managed to continue sending signals asking for assistance until just after midnight and then went silent. By two A.M., the last rifle and machine gun fire had died out. Beatrice had fallen.

Colonel Piroth apologized for underestimating his opponent by holding a grenade against his stomach and pulling the pin. From them on, each of the other strong points received its full share of the same treatment that had been given to Beatrice. Fifty-five days and nights of constant shelling and ground attacks took casualties, along with the rains that soaked everything and made the sandy walls of bunkers collapse, sometimes burying alive wounded men who didn't have the strength to get out under their own power. Reinforcements came in only to be swallowed up. There wasn't enough ammunition or medical supplies to handle half their number. Attack and counterattack, a strong point would fall only to be retaken an hour later. But inch by inch, man by man, the Vietminh gradually gained control, though not without cost to themselves. Over ten thousand died in the process, and over two thousand were taken prisoner and forced into labor gangs, to clear away debris and rebuild shattered fortifications and bunkers.

By the last part of April, nearly everyone knew they had no chance; but still they hung on in the hope that help would come. There were rumors that the Americans were going to supply enough planes to keep them reinforced and supplied and that a rescue column was on the way. Neither thing happened. Only the rains came, which in the months of March to August, average five feet. Tired men went to sleep and drowned in the bottoms of their bunkers or shell holes. Uniforms rotted on their backs, and feet swelled until they looked like fat, bloated, white maggots from which the hides were peeling off. They were losing fifty to a hundred men a day, and rations were cut in half.

The Viets taught the defenders something about digging. Trenches by the dozen crept closer to the defenders. Every day, some would go underground, trying to pass beneath the wire. Some of these were intercepted by the French sappers, who would dig until they intercepted the enemy. Strange hand-to-hand fights, with shovels and knives, took place under the soggy earth where the two groups of moles met to fight blindly as their comrades overhead fought with machine guns and flamethrowers.

All the outposts fell or were cut off from the main base, each left to its own devices. Casey could hear them on the radio giving each other encouragement, but one by one the radios went silent as their operators were killed or taken prisoner.

On April 13, Castries wanted to attempt a breakout, but his commanders convinced him that it would be a massacre. He gave in and ordered that at five-thirty the garrison would cease firing. Giap would be informed by radio. Until the last moment, the paras and legionaries fired off their remaining ammo and destroyed what was left of their serviceable equipment. They would leave nothing for their conquerors. At least they could salvage that much of their pride. Several bands tried for breakouts on their own, most of them to be captured or killed. At five-thirty, the Viets came out of the riverbanks of the Nam Yum River in thousands to swarm over the camp. A special squad went in to Castries' bunker to take him and his staff prisoner. From Isabelle, Casey could see the French tricolor go down and the flag of the Vietminh rise. Only Isabelle still resisted. LaLande, its commander, refused to give up, never, not while he still had men who could fight.

That night, his men, who were too badly wounded to come with them, gave covering fire to keep the Vietminh occupied. Those who could walk slipped out of the camp and down the bed of the Nam Yum and into the jungle wall. Casey was with them. Of the hundreds who tried to escape, only seventy made it back to French-held terrain. Most were from LaLande's group. While the victorious Vietminh made their own death march for the ten thousand prisoners they had acquired, Casey and the escapees were sent to Saigon for decorations. France needed some heroes.

It was over, and the French had lost. The Vietminh were given the whole of Tonkin. Cochin China and Annam were granted independence, soon to absorbed by the new masters, and Cambodia and Laos were demilitarized. Casey stayed in Hanoi until the prisoners of war were exchanged and loaded on troop ships, taking the Corps d'expéditionnaire away from Dien Bien Phu's defeat in the east to where another war of liberation was taking place among the colonies of France—back to Algeria.

A stomach twisting lurch of the plane as it hit a large air pocket stopped his reverie. Casey leaned back, shook his head to get rid of the past, lit up a smoke, took three deep drags, and butted it on the sole of his boot. Finally he let his eyes close, the lids were heavy and gritty.

CHAPTER EIGHT

They slept, tossing fitfully as the C-119 droned on through the night across the dark waters of the ocean, heading for the South China Sea.

The hours passed rapidly. Van woke first as the hydraulics signaled the lowering of the landing gear. He woke Casey and George as the plane banked to the starboard and began her approach to Clark Field.

The three men quickly strapped themselves in as the aircraft lumbered toward the runway. She bounced down like a fat old duck landing uncontrollably on a rough lake. There was a screech as the pilot reversed his props and rumbled to a stop. Then they were off again, taxiing off the ramp to the fuel trucks standing by.

Quickly the ground crew hooked up the lines to refuel the plane, as military guards took up positions around the aircraft to keep away anyone who might show an interest in the plane and its cargo.

As soon as the umbilical cords were detached, the plane taxied straight back to the runway with a priority clearance to groan and wheeze as it lumbered back into the sky. It still had a long way to go before it discharged its cargo into the night sky.

Several more hours' flight over black waters of the South China Sea brought them to the south of Phu Quoc island. From there the plane eased into its final heading.

The C-119 changed attitude to come in low over the

coast. Their ears popped with the change in pressure. The red night light in the interior of the plane gave everything a strange eerie cast. When the light came on they knew they were getting near the drop zone. The crew chief came back to them a few minutes later to say they had picked up the signal for their approach. It was time to get harnessed up.

The cargo master turned on the get ready light and opened the door to the outside. Casey hooked up his static line to the cable and stood in the open doorway watching the darkness race by him. Behind him, George and Van were ready to follow him out the door.

All at once, Casey felt the exhilaration he'd experienced in so many previous jumps and silently laughed at the awareness of how one always felt the need to piss after he'd harnessed up. It was no different now, but there was no time. They were fast coming up on the marker that Phang had set out for them: a burning arrow-shaped array of oil lamps showing the direction of approach. Now they were over it.

He threw his body forward into the jump position and tumbled out. Casey felt himself being tossed like a small toy. The prop blast was deafening. One thousand, two thousand, three thousand, four thousand, then a quick upward jerk of his body, and all was silent. The silence was always a shock after the ear-blasting roar of the engines. His hands moved quickly up to his lines, checking out the risers, an automatic movement of the experienced jumper. The touch told him that all was in order. The chute, billowing above him, looked too fragile to sustain his weight.

Behind him he could see Van and George dropping slowly. In the distance, the old cargo plane was visible only for a moment before going into a cloud and disappearing from sight. He adjusted himself and looked down. At night, depth perception was deceiving. Watch for the treeline, he remembered, and steered his chute closer to the clearing. The burning arrow had already fizzled, and only the light of a lone lantern showed the center of the field.

Casey drifted toward the light, seeing the tree line suddenly become a black shadow as the foliage blocked out the sky above him.

"This is it, son!" He braced himself for the impact, pulling his front risers down and releasing them. A snap! He hit the ground; the upward snap of the parachute helped to ease the fall. Casey quickly twisted his body into the parachute landing fall, or PLF, as they called it in school. Chin tucked, head down, knees together and lightly bent, toes down as he hit. Without thinking, he automatically went into his body roll, on the side of his calves, thighs, hips, and back and over.

His chute filled lightly, billowing with the ground wind as he rolled deftly to his feet and hit his quick release. Shadows grabbed his chute and collapsed it. An old and wrinkled hand grabbed his own and then helped him out of his gear.

"Welcome, my son! Welcome to Cambodia."

Casey put his arm around the old outlaw. "Phang, you'll never know how good you look to me, even if I can't see your ugly old face."

Looking over Phang's shoulder, he could just make out the forms of Van and George touching down, their chutes collapsing as Phang's men grabbed them, beating the silk to the ground and rolling them up. The two men quickly gathered their gear, gave the drop bags to the Kamserai, and joined Casey and Phang.

Casey took out his compass and took a sighting. The radium lit dimly.

"All right, gentlemen, silent running till we're in the clear. This is no time to take chances."

Pointing in the direction he wished to head, a Kamserai took the point. Indian style, in single file, they melted into the jungle. Setting a rapid pace, they weaved their way in and out of the trees and brush, putting as many miles as possible between themselves and the drop zone.

After about an hour's march Casey called a halt and had the natives bury the three chutes in the brush. Resting for a moment, he could almost feel the physical weight of the jungle bearing down on him. It had a taste to it, a flavor that was hard to describe, something all its own that told you, "You don't really belong here. Beware."

Casey rested his back against a tree, watching the shadows of the others as they did the same. Most of them faced to the outside in case unexpected visitors might come by. Sitting there, breathing in the dank heaviness of the myriad trees and heavy undergrowth, he heard a familiar sound that ran chills up his back and instilled a primeval spot of fear in his gut. The long, rasping, coughing sound of a hunting tiger. Not a roar but a cough, deep and throaty, a cough that a man could hear for miles. God, what a sound, Casey thought. It made a man feel damned inadequate.

He pulled himself to his feet, snapping his fingers twice to get the others' attention, and motioned for them to move out. They had to make some distance.

Van moved up behind Casey as George moved out to the right flank. Casey wasn't worried about George getting lost in the bush. The little shit could hear an ant fart at fifty feet. He would be where he was needed.

The Kamserai and their chieftain's foreign guests moved as swiftly as the terrain would allow, sometimes slowing to a crawl, making only a hundred yards an hour or less. Then it was time to rest. The gray light of the coming day was now bright enough to see one's hand before one's face quite clearly. He figured they'd better hole up and rest.

Casey, his men, and the Kamserai tribesmen blended into the underbrush, wrapping the jungle about themselves, invisible at a distance of less than three feet. They slept, all but the sentries. Their eyes never left the trail they'd just moved away from. They would sleep later. Now they would watch while the others pulled into their own special places in their minds and slept the sleep of the hunter and the hunted. Never fully asleep but never fully awake. A wrong sound or an abundance of silence would bring them to instant alert: no evidence of drowsiness, no rubbing of the eyes, immediate awareness, hands on weapons ready to kill if need be. These were the Kamserai, the hunters of men.

Some distance away from where the men in the jungle slept, another was disturbed from a most pleasant rest by the pounding at his longhouse door.

Pol Nar Lon, political leader for this district, swore beneath his breath as he rose and opened the bamboo door. A soldier of the Khmer Rouge stood outside at attention, his eyes downcast, waiting to be spoken to.

"What is it? Why have you wakened me?" Pol Nar Lon grumbled, instantly regretting the showing of emotions to an inferior.

The soldier swallowed, speaking rapidly in a voice that cracked from the dry taste of fear at being in the presence of the Colonel Lon. He informed him that the message in his hand had just arrived.

"Well, don't stand there holding it, fool. If it's for me, why is it not already in my hand?" Pol Nar Lon, colonel in the army of the Khmer, political and security chief of the district, was not noted for his leniency or tolerance. Deviation of any kind held only one reward, and that was best not thought of.

The frightened soldier handed his superior the written message just received on their radio from Phnom Penh and after a severe scolding by the colonel was dismissed. He was relieved that the potbellied officer had not asked his name.

Cursing all the peasants and underlings in the world, Colonel Lon slammed the door and moved to his desk. Ever since the central committee had assigned him as commander of this Buddha-forsaken post, he'd been tormented by the presence of small people.

He searched the desk area for his glasses. He was forever misplacing them. Perching them on his nose, he scanned the message before him, noting the seal of his commanding general. It had been a long while since he'd received anything of real importance from the esteemed general.

District Seven:

Office for Intelligence and Operations

1600 hrs. yesterday this station received information that an air drop was to be made in the region of Sien Dap village. Our informant states that this element consists of dissident Kamserai bandits and is led by an American agent for the CIA.

Subsequent information confirms that last night an unidentified aircraft was sighted in the vicinity of Sien Dap. Our records show that no authorized flights of any nature were made in your district last night. You will make every effort to ascertain whether there are hostile forces in your district. If so, they are to be taken, alive if possible, as their capture could prove of great value to our Ministry of Information.

> Signed
> General Surya Varman
> Intelligence and Operations
> for the Khmer Republic

Lon put the message down, looking at it long and hard for a moment. He smiled. This could be the break he needed. Success in this mission could bring his name to the attention of the Central Committee in the capital. If it was true that the foreigners were in his region, it would most likely give him national prominence to capture them.

He summoned his orderly and dictated a message to the general that he would take personal charge of the search and capture mission departing to the Sien Dap area immediately. With a wave of dismissal, he ordered curtly, "Go now to the radio shack and get it off to the general. On your way, tell Lieutenant Wen to rouse a company of our top soldiers for the patrol and rations enough for seven days, and also have my morning meal sent in. Go now, fool."

After his breakfast, Colonel Lon issued orders to his

adjutant to be on the alert for anything out of the ordinary and communicate the same to him in the field. The patrol would check back with the adjutant twice daily at 0700 and 1700 hours.

He went outside to where his troops were now assembled, waiting for his orders. The colonel could not resist a small premission speech to enhance his own image; perhaps it would also inspire his troops.

"Men of the victorious forces of liberation, the battle we waged against the capitalist army of America and her lackeys is not over yet. We are still not secure in our beloved homeland. I have this day received word that enemies of the state, led by an American no less, have possibly parachuted onto our land near Sien Dap. You can be sure that they mean us nothing but harm, so be ever on the alert while on this patrol. The man who first finds sign of their presence will be immediately promoted two grades. Be on the watch, comrades. Rest assured that they are armed and to be considered dangerous. I want these criminals taken alive if at all possible. Do not kill unless you are ordered to do so. You men are the bearers of the standard of the new order. Conduct yourselves as such, with courage and loyalty. Now, board your trucks!"

The men gave him one short rousing cheer and raced as one to their American-made deuce and a half trucks, remnants of the victory over the capitalists. The colonel went to the lead vehicle and climbed up beside the driver.

Someday, he thought, I shall have my own car, for me alone, and not have to ride in a damned truck like a fool peasant. He motioned for the driver to start his engine, and the column moved out toward the village of Sien Dap, thirty-five miles to their north, where the Annamite Range melded with the low country.

The chase was on.

CHAPTER NINE

Casey and the men woke up. They ate a meal of cold rice balls and *nuoc mam*, a sauce made from the bodies of fish. They stretched, scratched themselves, and relieved their bladders—all the things that civilized men do when waking. Then they moved out, heading for a mountain ridge overlooking a large lake some forty miles distant. If things went well, they would reach their destination the next day.

The combat patrol flankers were out, point man well in front, all weapons held in readiness and pointed to the side of the column. Casey had his first chance now to size up the men Phang had brought with him.

They were tough-looking men, all right. Wiry muscles like sinew twisted all over their bodies as if there were something alive under their skin, trying to escape. He had known that Phang would bring the best, and these certainly looked the part. They wore old American combat camouflage fatigues, uniforms that had probably been hidden and retrieved after the fall of the Saigon government. They carried a mixed bag of weapons: M-2 carbines, M-3 45-caliber submachine guns, and Chi Com AK47s. Two of the men were carrying SKSs, and all fifteen men accompaning Phang wore the ever-present homemade machetes and knives. A rugged crew of men for sure, a team that would give you nightmares if you were on the wrong end of their act.

Casey turned to Phang. "These men will do, old friend. You've done well."

Phang nodded, looking around in admiration of his troops. Van moved up beside Casey, reminding him to take a salt tablet; the heat of the day was starting to show itself. Casey asked where George was, and Van pointed to the outside flank. Casey could barely see the Montagnard's shadow, moving wraithlike through the trees and under-brush of the jungle. Members of the Montagnard company where he'd first met George used to call the little man "one who moves like a ghost," and they were not far from wrong. The wiry little bastard was a natural at this line of work and had taught Van and himself to be almost as good. They would never be his equal in the jungle, though. They'd started learning twenty years too late.

Colonel Lon and his men were at this time pulling into the village of Sien Dap. At one time, there had been over six hundred populating this small village; now there were but seventy-three. This was a town they'd been forced to make an example of. The populace had not been eager to accept the new order, and many of the men had served in the puppet army of Lon Nol as lackeys of the Americans. For that traitorous act, they'd suffered great punishment. The village had to be cleansed. The revolution could not make exceptions. Without emotionalism, the condemned members were taken to a pit outside the village—men, women and children, with no exceptions—and lined up. Only those families who had been totally loyal were spared. The machine gunners had adjusted the sights on their guns, fed in clean, shiny belts of freshly oiled ammo, pulled the cocking levers back, and fired. For two long, ear-shattering minutes the gunners had hosed the villagers down, hitting the jerking bodies with their deadly missiles again and again until no one survived. Not woman, not child. The party required that their soldiers be strong, but the gunners had cried, blaming their tears on the heat and smoke from the barrels that were starting to glow.

Finally, it was over. They shoved the bodies into the pit

and covered it over. The corpses alone had almost filled the hole. The troops had packed down the dirt and hurriedly left the area, avoiding each other's eyes.

Today, as the soldiers of the new order rode by the pit area, they didn't notice that the wind and rain had partially uncovered several of their countrymen buried there. The small tiny skeleton of a child's hand poked above the dirt like a fragile white crab, waiting. They had not seen it, and time would one day cover it again. The earth claims all sooner or later.

The villagers knew well how to respond to the colonel's questions. The lesson taught here had not been forgotten. Flowers and food were brought immediately for his men while Lon interrogated the surviving village elders. Had they seen anything? Any aircraft or strangers? What?

The elders nodded. Their young people had heard noises some time before dawn. One couple had left for the fields in the mountains, when they'd seen the glow of lights in the distance and had heard the sound of an engine in the air. They had returned now, just minutes before this great soldier and his men had arrived in the village. They had intended to send word of this event to him immediately, but the wise and honorable colonel had come before they could dispatch a messenger with the news.

Lon looked at the old ones with distaste, noticing their straggly white beards and lice-ridden clothing. They laid their clothing atop a red anthill every few days, he'd been told, and the ants would come to carry off the lice for their food. Buddha had not been kind to these people.

He ordered the young couple to be brought to him. A farmer of about twenty and his bride, a girl of perhaps fourteen, came and knelt before him. He enjoyed the feel of these people bowing before him: peasants in respect to their betters. Perhaps the old kings had known something about ruling. Enough of these thoughts, he reminded himself mentally. To work. Looking down at the girl's bared nubile breasts, he told the two to rise. The girl, noticing where his eyes lay, smiled timidly to herself. Perhaps these men in uniform were not so different from others. If she pleased him, he might be kind to them. Best, she knew, to let him look at her femininity and smile for him.

The colonel threw question after question at the pair, but nothing changed their story. They had nothing more to add to the fact that all they'd seen were lights that had been quickly extinguished and a glimpse of the plane before it had been lost in the clouds. There was no mistake; it was clear. Bringing out his map case, he opened to the chart showing their area and pointed out the location of the village to the young farmer.

"Show me where this field is!"

Colonel Lon gave him landmarks to draw references from. While the young man looked at the map, trying his best to understand the strange marks and their signifigance, the officer looked at his wife.

Finally, the husband pointed to a spot on the chart and indicated the location of the field to Lon's adjutant. His wife didn't notice that the young man had turned to look at the colonel's area of fixation. She was too busy handling her own emotions now. As the colonel's eyes fixed on her own, she felt a thrill go through her. Her nipples hardened, coloring a brighter pink, and protruded out at his gaze. A strange hot flash came over her, one she'd never felt before. Was it because this man was a chief, one who could have a person killed with a mere word? His strength and power of command drew her like the primitive she was—the urge to migrate to the dominant of the species. She felt her womanhood now more than ever.

The young man raised his eyes from Lon, moving to his wife, recognizing the look in her eyes as one of acceptance. His youth and pride betrayed his good sense. In anger, he struck his woman to the ground and turned to the officer.

"She is my woman," he blurted. "Tend to your soldiers and leave what is mine to me."

The colonel sighed, nodding his head to the bodyguard standing slightly to the rear of the angry youth. The guard raised his rifle and quickly struck the base of the man's skull. It made a sound not unlike that of a large eggshell breaking.

The guard apologized. "I didn't mean to hit him that hard, my colonel, but as you can see, his skull is very thin. A strong man's head would not have broken so easily."

Lon waved his explanation away.

"It is of no matter. We will leave shortly. Have the villagers feed our men, and do not disturb me until I summon you. Go!"

With that, Lon took the girl's hand and raised her from the ground. Without a word, she followed him to the longhouse of the village chief. As they approached, he ordered everyone out. As the frightened family hurriedly vacated their home, the colonel and his new woman entered without looking back. He knew she would be behind him. The laws of nature ran shallow in the forest, needing only to be teased a little to come to the surface. This was one of the basic laws of nature—to mate with the strong. As a female animal of the species, she went to the colonel. As a female, she gave herself willingly over and over, her husband already fading in her young mind.

Pol Lon finished with her, rose, and dressed, leaving her lying on the woven mats and blanket. Not looking back, he ordered his men to board the trucks. He left, leaving her to whatever comfort or pain the baby he had planted in her belly would give her; he was no longer concerned.

The trucks made their way along the dirt roads, throwing up clouds of red dust that settled on everything and found its way inside to coat their noses and throats till they had to take rags and scarves and tie them around their faces.

Heads bobbing, many of them slept as all soldiers can, no matter what they are doing. A bouncing truck was no problem. They dozed, occasionally jerking their heads up sharply as if they had had a dream of falling.

The clearing they were heading for was only ten kilometers across country from the village, but if they stayed on the road another forty kilometers, they would come within two clicks of the clearing and arrive there as quickly as if they had walked from the village. But this way they would be more rested.

Lurching, the lead truck came to a stop, almost making Colonel Lon smash into the windshield. The driver hurriedly began making excuses about how he had to stop suddenly to avoid a large hole. Colonel Lon did not, as the man expected, punish him. Lon was in an expansive mood. He had been dozing pleasantly, comfortable after his excursion in the village of Sien Dap. She was inexperienced but enthusiastic and eager to please; that compensated a great deal for her lack of expertise. He hoped the next man who claimed her would be properly grateful for the training he had given her in the arts.

Yes, she was pleasant. Perhaps another time.

He motioned the truck on and slid back into his light semisleep, letting himself reflect upon the many women he had known, the differences between them, from the sophisticated ladies of the city to village peasant girls like that one. They were all different yet the same. Laughing silently, he thought about the western woman, the Swiss sister he had taken when the Khmer Rouge took over the country. She was a missionary for some Christian church, another of those fanatics who felt some strange need to sacrifice themselves for a people they had no business interfering with. It seemed that the more of them that were killed, the more would show up beating on their ever-present Bibles, threatening you with the most vile punishments if you did not fall down and worship their pale Jewish god, as if there were not enough gods in this land already.

The party would be taking care of that situation. Religion sapped the strength of the people and needed to be controlled, as he had controlled the missionary. She had waved her silly book at him, saying that her god would punish him for this violation of her body. Even as she kept threatening, her body would move with him till finally her legs—and she had good ones—locked around his waist till he thought she was going to break his spine, and she began to buck and scream till she climaxed. Lon laughed at how her body had betrayed her. After he turned her over to his men, she lived through enough orgies to guarantee her a place either in hell or in heaven, depending on how much she enjoyed what was happening to her. But conscience is a terrible thing, and she'd hanged herself the third night. Lon often wondered why she waited so long to do it.

The capital. That was where to be. That was where the beautiful ladies were. If all went well, he would be able to get out of this pest-ridden jungle. After all, he had come from a good family and was used to the finer things. He had been one of Sihanouk's bright young men till the American CIA had him overthrown and that dog, Lon Nol, took over. Pol Lon had had to leave everything behind and join Sihanouk in China. While there, he had attended many of their schools—military training, psychological indoctrination courses, studies on population control and discipline. Most important to his Chinese instructors was a proper attitude. Loyalty and the ability to quote copious amounts of the never-ending wisdom of Chairman Mao were more important than intelligence. Lon quickly learned this and adjusted himself accordingly. Learning to spout Mao by the ream and always looking pious when his name was mentioned—this assured Lon of high placing when his instructors graded. He played his part even if it did bore him, but what was he to do? After all, he had no place to go and no money to go there with. Obviously, he had to align himself with the new forces that were coming into play in his country, and when the Khmer Rouge came to China looking for trained men, the Chinese instructors rated Pol Lon so highly that he was made a major immediately upon enlisting.

They had never asked whether he wanted to enlist or not, and it never occurred to him to question their assumption that he was as eager as a proper revolutionary spirit should be to go and throw himself on the bayonets of the revisionist running dogs supported by their capitalistic Yankee masters. The thought of throwing himself onto anything other than a bed or woman did not thrill Comrade Lon greatly, but he played his part and for his reward was given this asshole-of-the-world province to administer.

Perhaps that would change with the capture of these foreigners.

The spot was reached, and the trucks pulled over and unloaded the troops. He had them sort themselves out into their proper squads and gave the orders for the march, placing himself carefully in the center and removing his badges of rank. After all, an intelligent man did not survive by making himself an obvious target.

They entered the trees by the road, heading straight in, flankers out, weapons at the ready. They moved out, heading for the clearing.

CHAPTER TEN

While Pol Lon and his soldiers of the Khmer Rouge were approaching the clearing, Casey and his mixed group of outlaws were just entering the foothills they would have to cross to reach the range of mountains by the lake. At noon they stopped for another break. The heat of the day was hanging around in the mid-eighties, not too hot, but the humidity made them sweat heavily as they climbed. Rocky. You never thought of the mountains in Indochina as having rocks, but the suckers were damn sure here. At least this portion had its full share.

Up and up they went, feeling the straps from their packs cutting into their flesh, the muscles in their necks starting to burn in hot spots.

Lord, it has been too damned long since I've done any of this, Casey thought as he leaned his back against a tree to ease the burden of the pack.

Taking a pull from his jungle canteen, Casey motioned for Phang to come over. The old bandit jumped up and trotted over to Casey's position. What was it about him that reminded Casey so much of the Chinese friend who'd taught him so much about everything? Shiu Mao Tse! How many years ago had that been? The great circle . . . Shit! Must have been the old man's agility and tirelessness that reminded him of Shiu.

With no shortness of breath or any visible exertion at all, the old man sat down beside him.

"What is it you require, my young friend?"

Casey took a short breath and looked at the chief of the Kamserai. "You old fart, how the hell do you do it? I feel like I'm about to have a cardiac arrest, and here you are, bouncing around like a damned puppy. What the hell are you doing, overdosing on vitamins?"

Phang looked thoughtful for a moment. "What is this vitamins? Do you have need of it? If so, I will try to find you some, my friend. Are you hurt?"

Casey grinned. "No, you old goat thief. All I was doing was showing some honest admiration for you and thinking of how much I would have missed in my life had we never met."

Phang bowed at the waist. His affection for Casey had been proved time and again through the years.

Casey spoke again. "This trip will be worth all the effort, if for no reason other than my having the chance to watch you run circles around these younger dudes." He took care not to include himself with the others.

Phang nodded respectfully in acknowledgment of Casey's kind words and stated with great dignity: "I cannot deny what the gods in their wisdom have chosen to demonstrate through my body, poor and feeble though it is."

"Okay, you miserable polygamist, I acknowledge your superiority. But right now, I want you to find the man carrying my drop bag and remove my MG-34. It is about time we put her together. You never know when we may have need of her particular services."

Phang rattled orders in Cambode tongue, and one of his husky young men brought the drop bag over to Casey. Opening it, he removed the components. He assembled the gun in less than a minute, including the attachment of the fifty-round drum magazine. Casey liked the feel of this old weapon. He had fallen in love with this particular piece in World War II and still preferred it to any others he'd fired since.

It was kind of like buying a pistol at a sporting goods store in the States. You could feel ten weapons made by the same manufacturer and identical in all manner, yet you would still, after holding all of them, come back to the one that felt right in your hand. Something about it told you that this one was the one you should take. Guns, Casey knew, were personal extensions of yourself and should be cared for as such. A gun, like a man's body, if properly cared for would never fail you when you needed it; abuse either, and you never knew when it would cease to function properly.

That's the way it was with the old World War II machine gun for Casey. It fired eight hundred to nine hundred rounds per minute and had selective fire, semi or fully automatic. It weighed twenty-six and a half pounds, which seemed a little heavy at times, but when the weight was compared to the capability of the piece, it seemed light for the services rendered. The barrel could be changed in less than ten seconds. The Americans had borrowed the quick-change style from the Krauts, who had used it on their MG-42 during the war. It was a war that he personally had been trying to forget for a long time now, except for a few happy moments with Gus and Teacher.

Assembling the weapon, Casey felt the old thrill run through him again. He'd used the piece more than once since he'd taken it out of the Vietcong bunker in the Iron Triangle several years ago. He'd given it to George before he'd left the country instead of turning it in as a good soldier should. The little Montagnard had taken good care of it during his absence and was still toting it proudly when Casey had come back for him and Van in the hijacked plane.

He laughed, recalling their escape again. Phang looked at him questioningly.

After they got away from Nam safely, he had Harrison fly them to Kuala Lampur, where a group of Malays, in order to pay an old debt to Phang, had given them shelter and made the arrangements for their new documents. He mollified Harrison with the promise of payment later for his reluctant services, though it took a while. After Harrison got paid and a little time had passed for him to cool off, he had started to warm up to them a bit. They found out later that money had a most salutary effect on the Englishman, a passion that most men felt only for women. When they settled into K.L., he became a regular visitor. Though not a full member of their special club, he was given honored guest status so that he could insult each of them to his hearts content with impunity and affection.

Enough of those kinds of thoughts. He had a job to do. Time to get the show on the road. They'd been too lucky thus far. Something was going to go wrong; he could feel it.

He motioned for them to move out as he rose from under his tree.

Pol Lon and his troops approached the clearing that Casey and his crew had only recently vacated. As the clearing came into their view, visible now between the thinning trees, the colonel ordered his men into skirmishing positions, spread out and alert for any sign of movement. He ordered that word be passed among them to be especially watchful for evidence that people had camped in the area.

They moved out of the trees and into the open, slowly and steadily, not really expecting anyone to be there but wary just the same. His men had experienced some combat encounters that were still unpleasant memories. Even if all appeared to be safe and quiet, it was best to take no unnecessary chances.

They moved as one through the waist-high grass. They had traversed about half the field when the cry came to all ears.

"Here, comrades! Come and see." A young Cambodian on his first patrol had spotted something.

The Colonel barked his order: "Remain where you are! I want none of you to move and cover their tracks. Stay in position until I order otherwise."

Lon walked rapidly toward the young trooper, the elephant grass whipping against his breeches and making a swishing noise as he passed. Coming upon the young soldier, Lon looked down to where he was pointing at a spot on the ground. There was a cleared area of about three feet in diameter and signs of singed grass. He pulled some of the grass and smelled it. It had been burned recently. He called for his men to advance carefully and watch for more clearings like this one.

The troopers spread out and began their search. One by one, more spots identical to the first were located. Lon ordered one man to stand on each spot and the rest to move to the far edge of the clearing and remain there. He walked to a small rise not far from the clearing and looked down at his men, standing obediently on their spots. They formed an arrow. These spots had to be where the lights had been placed for the aircraft's approach and paratroop drop.

"Good," he said aloud. "They are here."

Instructing his men to fan out, he called for his scouts, two Meo tribesmen from Laos whom he'd brought with him when he'd come south. These men were the best trackers in the highlands of their country, and he'd been fortunate to obtain their services. If not for their families' mistreatment by a former royal Laotian officer, they would not now be in his service.

Pulling the two men close to him, he promised rewards if they found signs that would lead him to the strangers. The Meo nodded and went to earth, almost like hunting dogs. They felt and smelled the ground and then pointed in the direction Casey and his men had traveled. Not only the direction did they give the colonel but also how many men were in the party. Lon was pleased. He had the strangers decidedly outnumbered, and there would be no great contest when he caught up to them.

The time was high noon, and as Casey and his crew rested, Colonel Pol Lon, security chief for the district, was radioing the information that he'd acquired back to his superiors. He was in pursuit and would make contact with the invaders shortly. Deliberately, he did not disclose his location over the radio. He wanted no one else involved in this operation; it was his and his alone. Only he would receive credit for the successful completion of this mission.

"Go! Go!" he shouted to the two Meos. They were taking the point like well-bred dogs on the scent. They led the way, with Lon and his men following. The colonel intelligently placed himself in the center of his men. A commander must keep himself secure.

All that day, Lon whipped his troops into the pursuit, changing the point man every half hour, allowing the trail to be broken by a fresh trooper, setting the pace for the others.

While Casey and his men were forced to find their every step, Lon was having no difficulty following their trail. He was gaining on them with every passing minute of the day, and Casey was unaware that he was being followed. Finally, the dark shadows of approaching nightfall came upon them. Lon tried desperately to infect his men with his own sense of urgency, but with night also came exhaustion. They had to rest. But Lon knew that his enemy must also rest, and he was aware that he was fast closing the gap between them.

He ordered camp to be made. No fire. Cold rice would be their meal. Fires would signal their approach. No smoking. No lights of any kind. Light and sound carried far at night, and Lon didn't know how close they were. Silence and darkness was the command, and his men obeyed.

Less than five miles away, Casey and his men made camp. They were just across the valley on the opposite side of the hills separating them from their pursuers. He, Van, and George removed their ponchos and liners from the gear packs. The liners were lightweight. They were camouflage linings that were warm and could be used separately or tied to the ponchos to form insulated sleeping bags. The best damned things he'd ever decided to use for the field were these ponchos. Singly, they made a ground cover if the night was clear, or a shelter half. They formed a tent if two of them were connected together. Rolled up

with the liner, they were only about the size of a World
War II Kraut gas mask container. About four inches in
diameter and a foot long, they fit nicely on the belt at a
man's back, and they weighed less than four pounds.

Forming his two pieces of equipment into a sleeping bag
at first, Casey immediately changed his mind and disman-
tled them. Clouds were starting to roll in, dark and angry-
looking. They were in for a hell of a storm. He doubled up
with Van, a Kamserai doubled with George, and they
quickly formed two side-by-side tents from the ponchos
and liners. They all climbed inside and settled down for
the onslaught.

Casey smiled, hearing the sounds of George trying to
teach the young Kamserai how to shoot craps, and said
softly to Van: "It's a damned good thing we won't be
staying here too long. That poor Cambode won't have a
home or a wife to return to when George gets through with
him."

The storm came on dark and sudden. Angry clouds
broke open, and bright fingers of lightning searched their
way across the night sky. Casey lay, staring through a slit
in the tent flap, spotting the lightning flashes and counting,
trying to estimate the distance. What was the speed of
sound? Bit by bit, the storm increased in its intensity,
building up until the rumbling made the earth shake, as if
they were beside an artillery regiment, all guns firing
simultaneously.

The rain came down in big wet drops, sporadically at
first, then a solid sheet of wetness, wall-like, trying to beat
the forest down and drown the earth.

Casey knew that there would be flooding tomorrow in
the lowlands if this storm and its rains were widespread.
He'd sleep easily this time, knowing that the rains would
also deter anyone who might be interested in their arrival.
No one could move in this rain and keep his directions
straight, not even with a compass. By morning the spoor
left from today's trek would be wiped out, and no trackers
could follow. He felt better. With the rain cooling the

earth and dripping off the leaves of a fat banana palm to fall upon his poncho tent, he nudged Van in the ass to make him move over. Then he slept, letting the sound of the drumming rain take him into deep, untroubled slumber.

The night passed, and so did the rain, carrying itself farther into the north country, up into the highlands, where it finally exhausted itself, becoming nothing more than a belt of low-lying fog among the mountain ranges and burning off the day.

Casey woke with the first light. The Kamserai were already up and cooking breakfast. Like all good soldiers, with the coming of the rain they had carried dry wood into their shelters for the morning fire. They would have hot rice and peppers this morning and start their march with full bellies. Their fires made no smoke that was visible above the tree line, and if a wisp or two did rise, from a distance it would blend with the rising ground fog. The odor of the wood smoke made a pleasant combination with the damp smell of the foliage around him. It smelled good, but it made him uneasy. This was enemy country, and even if no one was aware of their presence, he was still edgy.

They ate, and Phang made sure the fires were put out and the ashes buried afterward. George came over to Casey, proudly displaying his new toy, a Chinese copy of the Russian Tokarev pistol. Casey commented that it looked like the old Colt .38 automatic, except that it had no safety. It sported wooden grips with a star emblazoned on each. It fired the Russian 7.62-caliber bullet. A good weapon. Not the best by any means but still functional. He warned George about taking advantage of the Kamserai soldiers, telling him that his life might depend on them later. George grunted that Casey never let him have any fun, but the thought stayed in his mind, and he soon returned the pistol to its former owner, considering his act a noble gesture. As Casey had said, it couldn't hurt to keep these bastards on your side.

Their small band broke camp and headed across the

valley, feeling their way over the slippery rocks, sliding a good portion of the way on dew-slicked leaves. Working their way through some brush, they came to a river at the bottom of the valley. Yesterday it had been a rippling stream that a man could have leaped across easily, but today it held an amazing resemblance to the Colorado River as it courses down the Grand Canyon, about forty feet wide, waist-deep and rapid as hell.

Casey, the heaviest of the entire force, tied a rope around his waist and made his way across. He fell once on the way, barely missing drowning through the energetic efforts of the Kamserai to save him. He'd start to get up, and they would pull him back down. Finally, regardless of their well-intended help, he made it to his feet, spitting out a mouthful of muddy water, and made it across without further incident. The Kamserai, meanwhile, were congratulating themselves on saving his life; surely he would reward them.

Casey tied the rope to a tree on the other side. He was sorely tempted to make a slip knot but resisted the urge. One by one they made their way across the stream, with some experiencing minor spills. Reassembling, they headed out again. One more ridge to go, then down to the basin to the lake and perhaps the cave of the Chinese family. Casey wanted to get out as soon as possible. He hoped they would find them on their first day.

His fatigues dried on his body as they marched, affording him some coolness for a short while as a small breeze blew up the valley from the south. Van took up a spot behind Casey as they moved up and over the crest of the ridge. Van thought about the first time he'd seen Casey and how their lives had become intertwined since.

He'd been assigned to a joint post in the delta, where he was working with a U.S. Special Forces team in Kien Thoung Province, one of the poorest and least populated regions of the entire country. It was strange to see so few people less than forty miles from the busy streets of Saigon. The province shared sixty-five miles of common border with Cambodia and had done so since the time of the Vietminh war against the French. A sanctuary for rebels and Vietcong, sitting on the northern edge of the plain of reeds, its lack of roads and the tall elephant grass made it almost perfect for guerrilla-type operations.

There were only a handful of Americans in the region at the time. In two years, they had established five camps from which to mount operations against the Cong. In each district were American Special Forces ''A'' teams, composed of three officers and eleven enlisted men each. They served to advise and assist their Vietnamese counterparts. Van had been one of these. He belonged to the LLDB (Luc Long Dac Biet) Special Forces. Between the Americans and themselves, they set groups, called the CIDG, or civilian irregular defense group, usually referred to as ''strikers,'' in each camp.

At Moc Hua, the province capitol, was the ''B'' team. They exercised control over the ''A'' team and provided assistance when needed. It was often needed. In those early days they had done much damage to the Cong. In the first six months of 1966 alone, they had killed over six hundred. In that preceding year the Cong had suffered losses equivalent to four battalions. Many caches of supplies were destroyed as the LLDB and the SF put them on the run.

But on Easter night, as the Americans called it, of April 9, 1966, the Cong commander had decided to change their fortune. They chose that night to win a victory that they sorely needed to offset their losses and show the people of the region that they were still a dangerous, wily enemy and a force to be reckoned with.

For the attack, the Cong commander had selected the 261st Dong Thap, the main force battalion, as the spearhead. They were reputed to be the finest in all Vietnam. They had been resting and training in Cambodia for some time, rehearsing their upcoming role in the war against the imperialists. They were to be supported by the heavy weapons company from the 267th Battalion and units from the 269th, both first-line Vietcong units.

During the lunchtime mess on April 9, the intelligence sergeant, one SFC Charles, had received input that an attack was going to be made on their camp, A-514, the forward operational base (FOB), a hundred-man position in the forward staging area. Van had been the Viet officer in charge at the FOB at the time.

Speaking to Charles on the radio, Van had wondered whether the information was true. They'd had many false reports of this nature, and they didn't have the manpower to react to each rumor that came down. But this time it seemed that too many things fit together. Certain similarities in today's input made him feel that this was the real thing. The last major attacks from the Cong had come on holidays, the Americans' Christmas and his Tet. Earlier reports indicated enemy movement along the border. All this put together had made his decision for him.

Team A-514 called its headquarters, B-14 at Moc Hua, and requested air strikes to be held in readiness, to be dispatched with the least amount of delay to any target designated. The Viet LLDB and the American SF prepared themselves meanwhile for an attack that was not certain to come. He'd been uneasy during the wait, just as he was right now, watching Casey's back and not knowing what lay ahead, to their side, or behind them.

The time had dragged by. Van was on watch at the FOB, and at 2307 hours the attack had finally set in. Mortars began to fall inside the FOB, with the Cong attempting to knock out the communications bunker and their main defensive weapon, a 60-mm mortar. It had begun to return fire as fast as the three CIDG troops could pass ammo to their gunner. The rapid reaction of the well-trained CIDG was unexpected, and the Vietcong attack had been slowed somewhat. They'd been attempting to get over the north wall but had fallen back. The CIDG had killed three VC and had wounded several of the others. Van had personally shot one in the face as he carried ammo to a gunner along their walls.

Another squad of VC infiltrated from the west. Undetected, they'd made their way under the cover of darkness, reaching the command post by their walls, and they had killed the radio operator. They were on their way back to the FOB when Van spotted the infiltrators from the west. A VC's back disappeared into their own communications bunker. He knew what was already happening inside and knew that he was too late to help his men. He rushed to within a few feet of the bunker door and took a quick look. He could see the radio man lying dead on the floor and the radio busted into pieces. The VC were going through papers and pocketing the code books from the desk. Van remembered now the startled look on one of their faces as he bent down to pick up some papers he'd dropped and spotted the grenade that Van had tossed inside now rolling between his legs. Van saw no more as he dove for cover.

After the dust had cleared from the grenade blast, Van entered the rubble and shot each VC in the head, just to be sure.

Outside, F-100 jets and AF C-47s had arrived over the FOB. During the time between the request for air and its arrival, the VC had let loose with their heavy stuff—recoilless rifles, machine guns, heavy and light mortars, including a heavy 50-caliber machine gun. The fight was on.

Van ran to where SSGT Rodney, one of the SFers on the FOB, was moving from one position to another, shouting instructions to the CIDG troops. Van told him what had happened to his radio. They would have to use the Americans'. From the amount of fire they were receiving, it was obvious that this was more than just a spoiling attack. There had to be more than a reinforced battalion hitting them. Van began spotting for the U.S. radio operator, Sergeant Roberts, pinpointing enemy positions for him to relay to the fighters and the Spooky, as the FC-47 was called. Spooky cut loose with its Gatling guns, pouring a burning hail of death in an arc over the positions spotted, sending six thousand rounds a minute pouring down. The speed of the plane and gravity were what made the rainbowlike arc of the falling thousands of bullets.

The F-100s started laying on some napalm. That and the heavy fire from Spooky kept the Cong from breaking into the small camp in force. By this time the only Americans left were Rodney and Roberts. The other SF had been killed by an infiltrator. A Vietcong suicide squad had taken the machine gun bunker on the west side of the camp and was pouring a concentrated fire on the CIDG positions, keeping them down and unable to return fire effectively. Spotting this condition, Van and Rodney organized a counterattack; while Van poured fire on the position, Rodney flanked it and came in from the outside the same way the Cong had come. They were not expecting anyone to approach from this direction. Their gun was firing out of the entrance into the interior of the FOB. Van kept their attention on him; then came a dull thumping sound, and a cloud of dust poured out of the doorway. It was Rodney's grenade. Lunging forward, Van and one trooper rushed to the bunker door, spraying the interior with automatic fire. They tossed out the bodies of the dead Viets and called some of their own men over to reoccupy the bunker, using the still-operable VC gun. About midnight a small group of Cong made their way up the northeast edge of the camp wall and began spraying with a Chinese flamethrower, setting fire to a barracks from which several strikers were firing at the Cong. The defenders were forced out by the flames, and Van put them into new positions to fire from. Van moved wraithlike through the smoke and dust, the flames from burning structures making scenes from Dante's Inferno seem altogether reasonable.

Van moved to where he could see the torch man, figuring that all things being equal, anyone who plays with fire must expect to be burned.

Van raced back to where he had stationed some of his men and took an M-1 grenade from them, emptying the clip. He had the Viet CIDG hand him some new rounds of tracers. Loading the piece, Van made his way back to where he could spot the Vietcong torch man who was having so much fun. The Cong flamer, illuminated by the fires he had set, was raised to one knee, looking for fresh targets. Van sighted by those same lights and aimed not at the man but at the tanks of liquid fire on his back. Grinning slowly, thinking, *Sin loi* (sorry about that). He took a breath and squeezed off the slack. The vintage 30-caliber weapon bucked, and before it settled back down, the Viet torch man was a running, screaming ball of flame, hands and face already charred black and shriveling, his eyes melting out of his head. If you play with fire, do not complain if you get burned, thought Van again.

Then the Vietcong began laying down rounds of white phosphorous with their mortars, igniting the USSF command post and knocking out the only remaining radio. When the FC-47 received no more directions from the ground, he began picking his own targets, using the light from the Cong's own tracers to spot them.

Enemy fire had almost stopped all friendly response at this time from the defenders on the east side of the camp. Spooky came in with all guns firing and reversed the situation in less than ten seconds of concentrated hell that he let loose on the terrified recipients of this deluge of steel and fire.

At 0100 hours the ''B'' team requested additional supplies and an armed helicopter platoon and any other fighters and Spookies they could get. From the last word they had from the defenders at the FOB, this was a big one and the allies' chance to waste one hell of a lot of Cong.

At 0130 hours a second group of F-100s came in, laying down sheets of burning napalm, providing a badly needed respite for the camp defenders to regroup and reorganize. That time was urgently needed, as several of the defenders' machine guns had become inoperable and Rodney and Van needed the time to cannibalize enough parts from the inoperable weapons and assemble one gun that was critically needed. At 0210, communications were restored by the dropping of a radio from one of the new Spookies. With the restored communications, the "B" team was informed that the Americans and their only surviving LLDB, Van, were still alive.

For the next two hours the fierce battle continued. Although heavily outnumbered, the defenders had blunted the first VC attacks and with the air support were keeping them from being able to capitalize on their numerical superiority. The defenders' steady and accurate fire was inflicting heavy casualties, and the number of Cong dead and wounded was continuing to mount. Lt.-Col. Williams, the U.S. Special Forces commander for the entire delta, had arranged for and personally accompanied a supply aircraft loaded with emergency equipment for the battered outpost. It arrived at Moc Hoa at 0310 from his detachment C-4 at Can Tho. Simultaneously, a platoon of armed helicopter gunships had arrived from the 7th Infantry division. A light section of two gunships was dispatched immediately to assist the FOB. One of the choppers had a hitchhiker, one Sergeant Casey Romain. Romain had been at the "B" team headquarters and saw the reports from the FOB as they came in. He knew they needed more bodies there; even one extra man might make the difference. Besides, he owed Rodney a debt. It wasn't too long ago that Rodney had pulled his ass out of the fire at Duc Co in the highlands.

The heavy section of choppers would be delayed slightly while they loaded with supplies and additional manpower for the post.

At 0402, Casey unassed the chopper, bringing with him an M-60 light machine gun and a half dozen belts of link ammo.

The first thing Casey saw when he leaped to the ground was a smoke-covered and smiling face of a South Viet officer wearing the insignia of the LLDB and speaking in a Cockney accent.

"I say, old boy, it is good of you to join us. Would you

care to meet the others? They are beginning to approach us now from the west wall, and I do so believe that you and your companion in your hands would have an interesting dialog with them.''

Casey had started to speak but could only stand, staring open-mouthed at the slant-eyed Englishman for a moment. He laughed loud and headed for the wall. Throwing himself behind some sandbags, he began to lay down fire from his M-60 machine gun. The Cong were taken by surprise, and several rows of their troops became twisted dolls in only a matter of seconds.

Van had nodded in approval at Casey's fire and said: ''Cheerio, old bean. Sorry terribly, but I must run now, though it looks as if you shan't lack for company during my absence. I see that more of the bastards are coming to visit you now. Well, I really must be off.''

Laughing, Van had disappeared, ducking, dodging, and rolling from one place of cover to another, until he was finally out of Casey's sight in a cloud of smoke. Van had sent one of his men to aid Casey, acting as his loader and assuring the unwelcome guests the same fate as the first ones.

At 0410 hours the heavy section of choppers arrived, bringing desperately needed supplies and ammo along with two more SF men, a Captain Rivers and a Captain Sheldon. They quickly unloaded their supplies and took up positions with the others inside the camp.

More reinforcements were on the way, he'd learned from the new arrivals. A relief and blocking force of company strength, accompanied by Master Sergeant Morion, Staff Sergeant Roberts, and Staff Sergeant Donaldson, had been dispatched from main camp toward Van's position at 0210 hours. The enemy forces had received a mauling and rightly feared that major reinforcements were on the way. They began a hasty retreat to the north and northwest, toward the Cambodian border. By 0500 hours, the badly battered enemy from the north was in complete withdrawal and had broken contact with their forward base.

Daybreak came slow and clear, almost startling to a man's eyes after the night. The light of day showed a picture of almost unbelievable destruction in the small camp. On the north wall there were but four men. Two of them were wounded and had set up positions in a ditch outside the wall. Four members of a Viet suicide squad lay dead in the inner perimeter of the camp. Their physical defenses had been ripped apart by the recoilless rifles and flames. Sixteen of the camp's defenders were dead, fourteen badly wounded, and three missing. His report would read one out of three KIA, WIA, or MIA. Three CIDG families were missing also.

Discarded and inoperative weapons lay all over the ground. Van was carrying one of his wounded to their new temporary aid station that had been set up in one of the machine gun bunkers, when he saw the sergeant who'd dropped from the heavens, Casey Romain, approaching with Rodney.

Van laughed now, staring at Casey in front of him, remembering his words as he'd spoken to Rodney: "What the hell is this guy, a Limey Viet?"

Rodney had laughed also, saying, "You'll get used to him. Van is something of a showoff but a damned fine officer. Van, this is Sergeant Romain, Casey Romain. He'll be with us for a while, I hope. I'm trying to get him assigned to our team."

Van and Casey had locked eyes then, and one of those rare cases of instant like and respect had taken place.

Yes, Van thought now, that Easter day had brought a few things to all of them. Most important to Van, it had brought a friend and comrade in arms.

The fresh troops had arrived shortly after that, and they'd all moved out in pursuit of the retreating Vietcong units. All in all, it was a bad day for Charlie, as his new friend, the scarred Sergeant Romain, called them.

Van grunted as he bumped into Casey's back, thinking

it was weird how one could lose oneself in daydreaming. Moving up to the side of his big-nosed friend, he looked down, following Casey's pointing finger. Casey spoke.

"The lake, Van! Tell the others to take a break now. From here on, we look for the family."

"Can they cook while they wait?" Van asked.

"Not yet. We still don't know what's out there. Maybe later, after we check everything out, we can all have some hot chow. Now, get a move on."

CHAPTER ELEVEN

Fifteen miles to the rear of Casey and his men, Lon and his troops made their way up the mountain on which they had spent the previous night. He was cursing his bad fortune. The rain had wiped out what little trail there was, and not even his Meo trackers were able to find it. Besides that, he'd spent an absolutely miserable night. The colonel often moaned privately about his frailties and delicate senses. In reality, he was as fragile as a water buffalo and possessed about the same soft and delicate sensibilities of one that was in heat. But he still moaned and swore at his men, driving them through the brush and searching for any signs that the invaders might have passed this way.

This was, after all, the general direction in which they'd been heading, and with any luck at all their trail would be picked up by his men again. He refused to let this one and only chance to get out of the jungle and obtain a nice desk job slip through his hands. He would keep these ignorant peasants searching this jungle until their babies were old enough to join them if it was necessary. He would find the enemy invaders, no matter how long it took.

The Kamserai troops, under Casey's orders, spent the rest of the day scouring the surrounding hills for signs of the Chinese family. It was late now, and Casey had received no word of their presence. If they were out there, they were damned sure laying low. He thought the situation over. Once he'd looked at it from their point of view, it was simple. The only way they were going to expose themselves was after being assured that they would not be harmed. How to accomplish that?

He reasoned that the only way they could let the family know they were in the area was to let their own position be known openly. That would also throw them open to any hostile elements in the area, but as it now stood, there didn't seem to be any choice in the matter.

Calling his men in from the perimeter, Casey walked the short distance to a cliff overlooking the valley and the lake. He stood there looking over the scene below him. Dusk was beginning to throw shadows across the sides of the valley as a cool breeze rustled the leaves and brush. The seemingly peaceful jungle was ripe, green, and lush, serene as the forests north of Rome. Yet he knew it was deadly, alive and teeming with thousands of animals and insects. Birds were beginning to fly in to nest for the evening. There was the equivalent of a swift change beginning to take place. One set of hunters, those who worked by day, were now coming in, while the second and generally more dangerous shift were just beginning to stretch themselves, to scratch and yawn. Soon they would go to drink at the clear waters of the lake and then fade softly into the dark wall of the jungle to hunt from their favorite places of concealment. They would wait there, some perched on branches, others lying belly to the ground. All had one thing in common. In order for them to live, others must die.

He took in the panorama below him and filled his lungs with damp warm air, calling out: "I am an American! I have been sent by your family to take you back with me to Taiwan."

Allowing time for the echo to subside, he waited a moment and called again: "We will camp by the lake. I will meet you wherever you say. Just let us know you are here. We have very little time to get you and your family out, Huan. Do not waste it!"

He'd used Huan's name; maybe it would help. However,

the enemy had been looking for them for some time, and they more than likely knew the man's name also. Now they must wait.

Across the valley floor, where the mouth of a small cave was carefully concealed by liana vines and roots of a teak tree, anxious ears listened to the words of Casey.

Turning back to his wife inside the larger room of the cave, Huan spoke. "Do you believe him, woman? I could not tell if the one speaking was an American or not. He speaks English as one."

A smaller shadow detached itself from the entrance and moved into the dim light of the interior, speaking with respect but purposefully.

"We must find out, my father. Soon our food will be gone. Let us watch their camp, and when it is dark, we will go close to them, to see and to listen."

Yu Li, nineteen, the daughter of Huan, knelt beside her father. The light from outside the cave flickered on her face as leaves moved from the stirring of the light wind. For one who was seeing her for the first time, it would be almost like a strike in the face, as if all the beauty of Asia were combined in this one small face. It was classic in its lines, and the blood of centuries showed in the set of her head. Hair, black and full as a moonless night, fell in a mass to below her waist. She looked at her father.

"We must know. If we do not, then the boys are dead anyway, or they shall grow up to be Khmer Rouge soldiers when the indoctrinators are through with them."

Huan sighed deeply. "I agree, my daughter. And you, woman, do you agree that we should verify the man's words?"

His wife was not fooled by the gruffness of her husband's tone. Years of love and a full life were not ruffled by the hardness of his voice. She knew that he was merely adopting this manner for the benefit of their sons so that they would not think him too soft on women.

She spoke in a quiet voice, respectful and knowing of

her position: "Yes, my husband. I agree. Time for us here is running out. We should know."

Her husband rose. "Then it is settled. Tonight I go and look at these men. The ones we saw from this distance did not look like Khmer Rouge to me. Yes, we will see."

At the same time Casey's voice fell on Huan's ears, another's ears heard his words. Not distinctly but well enough to take a sighting on. Colonel Lon eyed the direction of the voice, and a thrill ran through him. A primal instinct made itself known in the sudden eagerness he felt to pursue the voice. But the night and its darkness were catching up to them now. He would wait. No chances would be taken. Again he issued the orders. No fires . . . no talking. It was obvious now. The hunted did not know they were being pursued, and he preferred to keep it that way until the last deadly moment.

The night closed too quickly. The hunters rested, waiting for the first light of day, when they would rise and close in on their prey. Lon slept soundly, with no dreams. His men remained on watch in relays through the long night of the jungle, while up the valley, about six miles away, Casey and his men also rested, spread out in the brush by the edge of the lake, waiting for contact from the Chinese man or a member of his family.

The night was clear, and after the rain of the previous night, the earth was still moist enough for the light breeze to give them some relief. Casey had separated himself from the rest, telling Van and George to stay behind. He'd bedded down on the opposite edge of the lake, where the ground was free of brush. He'd thought about building a fire so that the Chinese could see them easily, but he was still leery that they might have company they were not aware of. There would be no fire this night. Maybe tomorrow, if they failed to show themselves tonight.

Taking his shirt off, he rose and went to the edge of the water, throwing handfuls of the cool liquid over his upper body, rinsing off the sweat and grime of the day. While he washed, his eyes watched. He finished and bent to pick up his shirt.

A voice hissed: "Move and you die!"

Casey froze in his bent position and whispered, "Huan?"

"Yes, it is Huan, white man. But how do I know you are what you say you are? Perhaps you are a Russian, working with the Khmer, out to destroy me and my family. I saw many Russians in China. You all look alike to me."

Despite himself, Casey chuckled at the old cliché. "Okay, Huan, just don't get trigger-happy. I'm going to get up now. The squatting position doesn't seem to agree with Occidental knees."

Rising slowly, Casey looked to the bushes, toward the direction of the voice.

"The man who sent us is your wife's father. He is now on Taiwan with his uncle, Lin Pao. We have just two more nights to get you out of here. After that it will be too late. Tomorrow a plane will fly over this position. We are to signal him, and he will drop the equipment we need to get you and your family out. What choice do you have, Huan? If I'm lying, you are a dead man anyway, and so is your family."

Huan thought this over. It was true what the man was saying. They had no other choice.

"Very good, American, if that's what you are. I will come out to you now. While you may be telling the truth, if you are lying, I promise I will take some of you with me. I was a soldier when you were still playing with child's toys."

Casey grunted knowingly. If he knew how old I was, he'd eat his own tongue for saying that, he thought. He stood, quietly waiting Huan's exit.

Huan came out of the brush carefully, facing the scar-faced and much bigger man. His rifle was slung on his shoulder, but in his hand Casey could make out an American-type MKII pineapple hand grenade, World War II vintage. The pin was pulled, and the man's hand was steady as it retained the striking lever. Casey paused for a moment before speaking.

"Good enough, Huan. I can understand your caution and why you're doing this."

He began to talk freely, giving the Chinese information that only his father-in-law could have known and passed on. He finally saw that he had the man convinced, and he relaxed as Huan put the pin back into the grenade. They both released a deep sigh and sat down side by side on the cool earth of the lake's edge. The strength seemed to leave Huan, as if his head were too heavy to hold erect any longer.

"Good! It is good. I did not think that Han would make so great an effort to save us. I care not for myself but for my wife and children. How will you get them out? The march would be too long and strenuous for the young ones."

Casey told him the plan, explaining what a skyhook was and how it worked. Huan nodded in agreement.

"Amazing! But you yankees are always making something work, even when it is not supposed to. I remember well the many machines that your soldiers were able to fix, machines that we were forced to leave behind when they would not run."

Casey's eyes went up in question. "Our soldiers? When was that?"

Huan laughed. "In Burma. I served with the 38th Chinese Division and fought beside some of your Colonel Merrill's men, on the road to Myitkina, when the Japanese held so much of my homeland."

Casey thought about that for a moment. "Then that explains how you were able to sneak up on me without my hearing."

Huan laughed softly. "No, my young friend. When you called out before night fell, I came to this spot before you. There are only two good locations to camp around this lake, and this is the best one. I gambled that you would find it, so I hid and waited for you. If you had not come here, I would have checked the other places."

"It's always a pleasure to do business with a professional." Casey grinned with respect. "I have a feeling that you're going to make this job a lot easier for me, Huan."

Huan bobbed his head in acknowledgment of the compliment.

"Thank you, big one. I do believe that it would be prudent for us to go and meet with the other members of my family. Women, it seems, always worry when their men are out of their sight for more than a few minutes. Go and speak to your men. Tell them to remain here while you meet with my wife and children."

Casey agreed and returned to the camp, putting on his shirt as he walked. Going over to where George and Van were talking with a couple of the Kamserai, he told them what had occurred and indicated that he was to accompany Huan to the cave. Van and George wanted to go along, but he told them to stay and keep an eye on things in the camp and to pass on to Phang what was coming down. He saw Phang then, squatting not far away, and decided he'd tell him personally. The old man added some *nuoc mam* to his rice and took a bite as Casey filled him in. He wiped his mouth on a sleeve and spoke.

"It is good that we have found them so quickly. One of my men was scouting our back trail and said he spotted a light, as of a cigarette."

"How far back?" Casey asked.

"About five or six miles from this place. The man was not certain of the distance. You know how hard it is to estimate distance in the jungle at night, my friend. A glow of a cigarette can be seen for miles and seem like a few hundred yards."

"Okay, old friend. This is how we play it. I'm going to get the Chinese family. You get your men ready to move out. We travel tonight. When we leave the area, we will also leave a good trail for the ones behind us to follow. If they are Khmer troops, we have to get them away from this area. The plane comes tomorrow night, and we must have them away from here. Let's take them for a phony run.''

''Wait a minute, my impetuous friend, and listen to this old and useless man. With the children it would be difficult to set and maintain a hard and fast pace. Would it not serve as well for the ones behind us to only think that we had all left and were heading away from here? Would it not be best for you and your two men to remain here with the Chinese in their cave while me and my men lead the strangers behind on an extended tour of the countryside? I am confident that we can lose them and then rejoin you here tomorrow night.''

Casey thought it over. The old bastard was about as useless as a twenty-year-old genius. ''You're right, wise one, though I don't like having you take all the risk alone.''

Phang laughed low, his voice guttural. ''My son, I was fighting in these hills before your father cut his milk teeth. Now show me the place where we shall meet.''

Casey laughed also. Why was it all these young bastards thought they were older than he? He took out his silk map of the region that Major Shan had made up for him and pointed to a clearing about five kilometers north of the lake.

''This is where we will be. If things go well, we will have them all out within one hour after the plane drops our lift equipment.''

Phang nodded. ''And what of you, my friend? Will you also leave the same way, hanging like a fish from a hook?''

''Yes, Phang. We get them out first, then me and the boys go the same route. you and your men will give us cover and then take off for your own safe area. I will arrange the final payment to you as soon as we get back to Taiwan.''

Phang grunted. ''I did not speak of payment. I know you will see that it is taken care of. But I am glad that you will be going out with the Chinese. It would not go well for you if you were caught in these lands.''

"I know,'' Casey said. "So we will play it your way.''

Leaving the old man to his unfinished rice and fish sauce, Casey returned to Huan. "Okay, let's go.''

On the way to the cave where Huan's family waited, he filled him in on Phang's suggestion that he stay with the family while the chase went on.

"What about the other two men? You say they will also stay behind?'' Huan asked Casey.

"They will be waiting for us in another spot. I don't want us all cooped up in the same location if things go down wrong. I told Van and George to leave tonight and find a hiding place close to the pickup spot. They'll be there.''

Huan nodded, accepting Casey's plan. "That is wise, my newfound friend. As you yourself said earlier, it is good to know that one is dealing with professionals.''

They made their way through the brush, taking exceptional care to leave no sign that they'd passed through. As they worked their way to the ledge and the cave where Huan's family waited, Casey felt uneasy. A growing itch inside that told him things were going too smoothly. They'd had it too easy up to this point. Something had to go wrong. It always did.

Eight kilometers behind Casey's location, another was not having it so easy. He was finding out the consequences of being derelict in duty.

"Kill him! Kill him quietly!'' Lon ordered. "Anyone so foolish as to light a cigarette when on patrol does not deserve to live. Take this fool away and strangle him.''

The young Khmer soldier who'd lit up without thinking broke down, throwing himself at Lon's feet and begging for mercy from his commander. The colonel looked down at him in disgust.

"Young man, you could have caused us failure this night. You have no idea what that thought does to me. Believe me, having you strangled this night will not be unkind. It will be a kindness compared to what I would have done to you if you lived and I found out for certain that your stupidity had alerted our quarry.''

The youngster began again to plead for his life. Lon motioned to the man standing over the kneeling soldier. Taking his AK-47, Lon's bodyguard, the one who'd disposed of the ill-mannered villager, struck the young Khmer at the base of his spine with the butt. The young soldier reared back, his spine and neck stretched taut in an arc of pain. Before he could scream or protest, the rifle strap of the AK-47 was wrapped around his neck. The guard quickly spun the weapon as if it were a small baton, tightening the leather strap like a garrotte around the neck of the teenage soldier. The victim went into a spasm for only a second, his legs and arms trembling uncontrollably. Then came a sound like the breaking of a one-inch piece of green wood. The boy's neck snapped, and his trembling ceased.

Propping the body up against his knee, the guard unwound the strap, easing the pressure on the youngster's neck. As he did, for a moment it sounded as if the boy were still alive. The air trapped inside his lungs escaped, hissing with a light rattling sound.

Lon nodded his approval. ''Very good,'' he said to the guard. ''You surprise me sometimes, Souvang. You really have a creative imagination in some directions. Good. Quite good.''

Colonel Lon did not rest well that night. The thought that the young fool's carelessness might have warned the invaders of their chase tormented him so much that each sound from the forest grated on his nerves like a jagged fingernail on a chalkboard.

CHAPTER TWELVE

While Colonel Lon tossed restlessly, Sou Phang and his warriors broke camp and headed into the black of the jungle. The trees overhead were like a canopy, shutting out all light.

The Kamserai and their chief made their way as quickly and quietly as possible, careful to leave a trail that was not too obvious yet easy to follow for trained eyes. Step by step they made their way through the dense undergrowth of the jungle, away from the area of the drop zone. Before the sun rose, Phang wanted to be at least ten to twelve miles from the lake.

Casey followed Huan's figure into the opening of the cave. It took a moment for his eyes to adjust to the light inside, dim though it was, coming from a rusty but functional lantern. When he was able to focus, his eyes fixed on a figure in the rear, leaning over her two small brothers protectively. Yu Li's face was framed like an artist's portrait, her hair hanging loosely on the side, its blackness setting off her skin like fine ivory. For Casey, the sight of her was like stepping into a cold shower, almost a physical shock.

Seeing the shocked expression on Casey's face, Huan chuckled.

"I know what you are experiencing, my young stallion friend. It is often that I wonder how one like myself could have sired such a beauty. But let me warn you, she is as stubborn as she is beautiful. I am sure that is why she is long past the age to marry. But you know how these modern women are. Come now and meet the rest of my family, members of my life.''

Casey walked over and knelt by Huan's side. The sire of the small clan made the introductions. Huan's wife smiled and bowed, asking if she could fix him tea or something to eat. Casey had been hungry before, but the sight of Huan's daughter had erased all thought of food from his mind. Forcing himself to stop staring, he looked away.

Yu Li, now that his eyes were not on her, had an opportunity to study this stranger. When his eyes first fell on hers, she experienced a strange and pleasant chill. He was not like other men she had met. She felt it immediately. He was strong and masculine. As she looked at him now, she could feel the violence in him. Violence but not cruelty. Yet beneath the violence, she also felt there was gentleness, a gentleness that was almost begging her to show it how to escape from its captor. She was certain that in time she would show it the route.

Huan explained to his family what had transpired and what the morrow would bring for them. He omitted the skyhook part, not wanting them to worry about the un-known. He would explain the function of the pickup equip-ment to them tomorrow. Now all must rest.

Huan turned the lamp low, leaving them only enough light to see one another vaguely. They slept. Yu Li was beside her brothers, with her back to Casey. Casey leaned against the cave wall in a sitting position, his back com-fortable against its coolness. He let his eyes fall on Yu Li's back, resting there, not knowing when they closed.

Dawn came, and while Phang and his men moved through the jungle and brush, Colonel Lon's men were up and on the trail. In less than two hours they were at the Kamserai lakeside campsite. Lon's Meo trackers bent to sniff the ashes, purposely left there by the others, and moved in circles until they'd decided on the direction Phang and his men had taken. They informed Lon that the invaders had left some time the previous night.

Lon swore, recalling the young soldier he'd had strangled. A lucky boy to have died so swiftly, he thought. If he was here now, I would feed him his own testicles.

He whipped his men into action, urging them onward and after the invaders. Mile by mile, using his men in relays to break ground, he pursued the unseen enemy. As they crested a hill, he instructed his radioman to contact headquarters and inform them that he was hot on the trail and closing in on the enemy force.

Phang rested his men for a while. He spoke to one of them. "If the Khmer dogs are following, then it would not hurt to reduce their numbers. Is that not true?"

The Kamserai grinned, showing long yellow teeth. "Agreed, father of us all!"

Still grinning slyly, he left. Taking two others with him, he went back down their trail, carrying a small rucksack. Selecting a likely spot, they went to work, setting up a daisy-chain booby trap with hand grenades. When the wire was tripped by the point man of their pursuit party, five grenades would explode at intervals to his rear, killing or wounding some of the troops behind him. They were exceedingly careful to leave no sign of the trap, except for the trip wire. They set the wire where the trail narrowed and then put a piece of torn blanket on a jagged edge of a broken tree. Whoever passed this way, his eyes would automatically be attracted to the trail sign of the cloth and away from the wire at his feet. Finished, they scanned the ground immediately around the trap for any signs they may have overlooked. Satisfied that there were none, they returned to their fellow tribesmen and informed Phang that all was in readiness.

Phang nodded approval. "Good! It is good. Now the dogs will follow much slower. Now we shall return to my friend and his family in distress and make sure nothing happens to hamper his departure."

He waved his men to their feet, and they again took to

the trail, leaving five steel balls of death on their back trail, eagerly awaiting the Khmer Rouge.

While Lon and his troops headed up Phang's trail, Casey and his small party were heading for the drop zone. An hour ahead of them, Van and George waited at the edge of the DZ, eyes alert. Van unslung his G-3 from his shoulder and broke it down. It was always smart to take care of one's weapon when one had a chance. The process of breaking it down, cleaning it, and then reassembling it took no more than five minutes from start to finish. George contented himself by eating a handful of last night's rice, cradling his shotgun on his lap. His shotgun was not as intricate as Van's rifle. They waited for Casey and the family to arrive, sitting at the edge of the clearing, waiting and watching, tired but alert.

Colonel Lon halted his troops briefly to confer with his Meo trackers. Grunting, they told him that they were no more than two hours behind and closing. They were gaining on the target and should catch them by nightfall. Lon smiled in approval.

"Good! Good! Then let us get after them. We must have them in our sights before darkness falls this night."

His men fell back into line formation. Lon was tired, but as long as he could march, his men would follow. They did. The lead Meo guide made his way rapidly along the easy trail. His eyes caught sight of something off to his side. It looked like a piece of cloth, maybe ripped from a backpack in passing. He moved over for a closer look. His bare toe felt the wire; and without thinking, he threw himself to the side of the trail, face down, hands covering his head protectively. The warning cry that was only now breaking from his lips was immediately drowned by the dull repetitive explosions coming from behind him on the trail. Before the vibrations of the exploding grenades had faded, a chorus of screams had set in to take their place. Two lay dead, and three were wounded beyond marching capability.

Lon cursed his fortune as he whipped his men on. He

left one medic to do what he could for the wounded. Damn them! They know we are following, he thought. He urged his men on, not letting them exercise more caution. The two Meo trackers slowed, eying the trail carefully, but Lon called one of them to him, telling him of the fate that awaited him and his companion if they didn't hurry. They chose to hasten, more afraid of Lon's wrath than of the possibility of more booby traps ahead.

On a ridge across the valley, Phang and his men could hear the distant thumping of the exploding grenades. He smiled knowingly.

"Good, my children. We have wounded the dog. He will go slower now." Phang didn't know how wrong he was. Lon would not slow down. Phang, without the aid of a compass, pointed his face unerringly in the direction of the drop zone. "This is the way we go now, my sons. Hurry!"

Colonel Lon stumbled and fell in his haste. He lay on the ground, his chest heaving and aching for breath, his face dark with anger and exhaustion. Why, he wondered, had they done it? If they knew we were following, they must also be bright enough to know that their trap would let us know they were on to us. They could have made better time without letting us know. They could have better covered their trail. Cover their trail? That's it! We have been following too easy a trail. It was left by them to lead us away. But from where? Where did they first learn that we were following? The lake? Yes! The lake! It must be the area that they did not want us to linger at. That must be where whatever is to happen will take place.

Pulling himself to his feet with the aid of a hanging liana vine, he turned his men back down the trail the way they'd just passed. "Hurry," he screamed, "to the lake. Back to the lake. We must hasten!"

They raced, with several of his men falling beside the trail, hearts almost breaking from the strain. But Lon would not wait. He ran, and his men ran. Infected by their commander's intensity, they entered a fog, dazelike, an unfeeling denseness like Olympic runners feel when their minds seem to leave their bodies and one foot is placed automatically ahead of the other until reaching their goal.

They ran, many of them slowing down to vomit and then running even faster to catch up to the rest. Their footsteps, in unison, seemed to say, "The lake, the lake, the lake." When they reached the lake, they would rest.

Casey came upon the clearing, with Yu Li following closely. Once, back down the trail, he had stopped suddenly upon hearing something, and she had bumped into him, her breasts flattening against his lower back. He'd felt the warm, full pressure of them and would have liked to find reason to stop again the same way. Would it seem too obvious to her? He didn't know that Yu Li was hoping he would try again.

How strange, she thought, that just to touch this new man could bring strange flashes to her thighs and loins. It was at this moment that she decided to take this man for her own, and Yu Li was used to having her own way. Yes, this was her man, the one she'd been waiting for.

The six of them entered the clearing slowly, cautious eyes scanning the far side for any movement. He'd seen signs to indicate that Van and George had passed down the same trail he'd taken, and he knew that they were around somewhere. Casey stepped from the brush and into the open, ready to jump back to cover if anything went down. He felt a sigh of relief escape his lungs as the figure of George raised itself from the waist-high grass and waved him over.

George called softly, "Over here, Trung Si."

Casey told Huan and his family to remain in the treeline and walked over to George's position. "Where's Van?"

"Van go to look around, Trung Si. To see that no Cong come here."

To George, all enemies were Cong, no matter what their race. Casey had tried more than once to explain the difference to George, but he'd given up when George had asked what the difference was as long as he knew personally whom he was speaking of.

He returned to Huan's location. Kneeling, he told them to rest and feed the children. It would be getting dark in two more hours, and if there were no problems, the plane would be overhead.

He left them, going in search of Van. Phang and his men would be arriving soon, and they must plan their perimeter defense to protect the family and the supplies that would be dropped. Possibly they had landed undetected and no one was looking for them. He doubted it, though, and it was better to be prepared for the worst than to be caught with your drawers down.

He could not get his mind off Yu Li. Damn it to hell, the little shit was beautiful. He hadn't seen anything to compare with her. Not even the dark-haired beauties of Rome could touch her. Why was he avoiding her eyes? he wondered. What was it about her that made him feel like an overgrown, inept schoolboy? His loins ached just thinking about her. He forced her from his mind when Van stepped from behind a tree to his side and damn near scared him to death.

CHAPTER THIRTEEN

While Phang's Kamserai raced for the clearing, Pol Lon and his troops sprinted for the lake. At dusk both parties reached their goal: Phang at the field, where he was met and greeted warmly by Casey, and Lon at the lake, where his men fell exhausted into the cool waters and drank. Many threw up and then drank even more of the sating liquid.

Lon raised his eyes from the water's edge. Almost as if it were too distant to hear, not certain that it wasn't the beating of his own heart, he heard a throbbing sound, now growing gradually stronger. Now he was sure. A plane! A big plane was approaching. His men were silent as they listened to the droning of the engines.

"There." Lon pointed. He could see it now; it was a large cargo-type aircraft, flying low to the ground and off to the right of their location.

Lon quickly removed his map from the case and looked carefully over the surrounding area. There was only one clearing of any size in this area, and it wasn't large enough to set down a plane of any great size. At any rate, it must be where the invaders were located, waiting for their plane. But for what purpose? he wondered. What could they have accomplished in so short a time? Could more troops be arriving with the aircraft? Or supplies? Yes, they must be at the clearing. No other place made sense.

Getting his men to their feet, he moved them into the

111

trees. At a double-time pace he herded them toward the clearing and what he hoped would be the lair of his prey.

"Hurry," he screamed. "Hurry! They must not escape." He was avid, eagerly anticipating closing in for the kill. He would have their hides nailed to his door before the morning meal tomorrow.

The C-130 was heard by the Kamserai before Casey had caught the sound of its approach. It was right on time. Major Shan was right on top of the operation, Casey thought, mentally forgiving the good major for a number of real and imagined offenses.

George took the radio entrusted to his care by Casey out of its case and handed it to his boss. Casey hit the talk button.

"This is Romain, do you read me? Over."

"Yes indeed, Yankee, we read you five by five. Are you ready for your drop? Over."

"Roger!" Casey responded. "On your next pass, come in from the same direction you just did. Drop the gear as soon as you clear the trees on your side. The wind is out of the south-southeast, about ten knots. Do you roger? Over."

"Roger, round-eye, here we come. Out."

One of Shan's wiseasses. Casey smiled. "Hey, Van, do you have any relatives in the Chinese Air Force?"

"Certainly not," Van replied indignantly. "There ain't no chinks in my family tree, boss." He too laughed.

Huan left the treeline, entering the clearing to stand beside Casey. "Is there anything we can do to help you?"

"Not right now, Huan. It would be best if you stay with your family. Keep them happy; reassure them everything will be fine. Okay?"

Huan nodded, returning to his people. Casey could see him talking to them, all heads nodding, their eyes wide with excitement as they turned to watch the events in the clearing.

The C-130 was on its approach now. Casey saw the drop doors opening. Like mushrooms, four small parachutes broke free from the plane and floated to the ground.

Good drop, Casey reasoned, dead center of the clearing and none in the trees. He keyed the button again, talking to the plane.

"Orbit this position for twenty minutes. If I don't call in any changes, use the same approach for your pickup."

"That's a roger, Yankee. We are at your disposal."

Everyone except the Kamserai on guard around their perimeter raced for the chutes, collapsing them as fast as they hit the ground, dragging the bundles into position in the center of the field. Breaking them open, they removed the individual kits. Casey had the bundle with the balloons. He handed them to Van and a couple of Phangis warriors, telling them to fill them. He called Huan over and told him to prepare the two young boys for the pickup. They would go up first. Huan called to the boys. They came running, eyes wide with expectancy, and stood by the two men.

After a few words from Huan to his boys, Casey started to harness them, asking Huan to translate for him. This was to be the greatest ride of their entire lives, he said. They were to sit down, putting their heads on their knees, and wrap their arms about their legs, holding them there as tightly as they could. They would not be harmed, Casey assured them. And just think of the story they could tell their relatives on Taiwan. All of this Huan relayed to the youngsters, adding a small amount of encouragement of his own. They were his sons, and it was time for them to act like good soldiers, following orders and being brave. The two boys grinned at each other, a frightened and tight-lipped grin but a grin just the same. They would do, Casey thought.

Casey adjusted the harnesses to a tight fit, snug but not too snug. He walked them to field center, where Van had one balloon fully gassed and ready. He pushed down on their heads, forcing them into the sitting position as their father had prepared them to do. Van's balloon was rising now. The Kamserai were holding tightly to the balloon's retaining lines, acting like children with a giant balloon toy. Up it rose, to a height of a hundred fifty feet. The boys were seated and in position, four feet apart. Casey hooked the youngest one to the balloon line. He was too light.

He called to Huan. "Get the other boy over here, too. This little sucker is too tiny. We'll send them up together."

He sat them back to back, connecting the line to both harnesses, and tied their straps together with extra line.

Huan looked worried, glancing from the boys to Casey's eyes, and then to the treeline, where his wife was biting her knuckles worriedly.

"They'll be okay, Huan. Don't worry. This way they'll be together and less afraid." They didn't look at all scared now, at least to Casey.

He keyed the mike on his radio. "Okay, you Chinese von Richthofen, this is it. You're picking up the children first, so be extremely careful. Come on in and get 'em. Over."

"Roger on that, Yankee. No sweat. We were the group with the highest score on this operation at Fort Bragg. Here we come. Out!"

The plane swung wide for a long approach, its engines straining as the props reached for more air. The V-shaped catching device on its nose was beginning to line up with the ballon. They came in then, throttling back as the line was snagged. The two boys seemed to sit still for just a moment. Then they were up, rising absolutely straight for a distance of about sixty feet, pausing there for an instant, and then taking off in pursuit of the plane, looking as if they were chasing it. The air crew started to wind the winch, bringing them in to the aircraft. Huan looked as if he were breathing a little easier.

The radio snapped at them. "Okay, Yankee. It was a clean catch. Get your next one ready and stand by. We'll return in a moment. Do you roger? Over."

"I read you, Chinaman. They'll be coming to you one at a time from here on and—" He was interrupted by Phang's frantic yell.

"Khmer Rouge, Casey, Khmer Rouge. They are coming!"

Oh, shit, Casey thought, we're in for it now. Why couldn't the bastards have waited another hour or so? He yelled at Phang: "How far away are they?"

"About one-half kilometer," came Phang's reply. "Will you have time for completion of your pickup?"

"Hell, I don't know. How many are there? Will you be able to hold them back for a while?" He knew before he spoke the question that it was too much to ask. They'd need all the help they could muster, and besides, the Khmer would probably be shooting into the air at the escaping pickups as they rose. Phang answered his question.

"There are about seventy-five of them. We can hold them for a while if they do not flank us. I don't have enough men to cover the entire area."

"Okay," Casey barked, "this is how we'll handle it. Set booby traps. Grenades with tripwires, whatever you can rig up." He called the plane. "Okay, Chinaman. You've picked up all you're going to get from down here, at least for a while. We got some unwelcome company coming. Are the kids okay?"

"Roger, Yankee. They are A-1 shape. Any message for our boss?"

"That's a roger, Chinaman. Tell him to try and contact us farther south in three days. We'll need that much time to shake off these dogs following us."

"Roger, Yankee, straight south on this same approach. We will keep our ears open. *Ding how*, Yankee."

Casey turned to Huan. The wife and daughter stood close by him. "Huan, we've got to run. Can your women keep up??"

Huan nodded. "Yes, they are strong, my friend. And they are Chinese. They will do what we have to do."

"Good enough! Get them into the center of the line as we move out. Oh, and tell them not to worry about the boys. They'll be in their uncle's care tomorrow." He turned to the Kamserai chieftain. "Phang, get the flankers out and into position. George will take point. Van, you stay with the women and Huan. They represent a considerable amount of money to us, so watch 'em close. Besides that, they deserve a break.''

Phang's men raced in from the trees, shouting that the Khmer were only a couple of hundred meters beyond the treeline. "Move 'em out, George! *Di, di.*''

George took the point, leading them into the southern edge of the trees, heading south. The skies were beginning to glow with the coming of night. That was their hope, Casey reckoned. Losing their pursuers at night should be relatively easy, giving him time to figure out what to do with them tomorrow. Phang had assured him that the grenades were in position behind them. That would slow their pursuers a bit.

The wall of trees closed in behind the last of the Kamserai bringing up their rear.

"Faster," shouted Lon Pol. "Faster! We almost have them.''

One of the Kamserai soldiers pointed up the mountain. Barely visible in the distance was the pickup balloon. "What is that?'' he asked his colonel. "A balloon? Why?''

Then the C-130 made its pickup. Lon saw the dark bundle being raised into the sky and following the plane.

A skyhook, he thought. That's what it is. A skyhook! I saw pictures in China of this operation. That was how they intended to make their escape. He turned to his men.

"Quickly, you dogs! Quickly! They must not escape me.''

He whipped his men onward, to the area of the balloon, through the oncoming shadows that said that night would be on them soon. His point man sent word back that he could now see the clearing. One of his men, shortly upon their arrival in the now desolate area, yelled to his commander that he'd found something. Lon headed in his direction, just able to see his man standing over a bundle. As he hurried, he yelled a warning to the soldier not to touch anything. Before the yell had cleared his lips, the man had already bent down, reached inside, and raised the dim mass. Lon's warning was too late. He watched as the curious Khmer Rouge soldier disappeared in a blinding flash of helium fire, ignited by the grenade that had been placed in position beneath the bundle and under the tank. Its handle had been set to go off if the tank was moved at all, releasing the awesome explosion and devastating blast that would destroy anything in its range.

Lon fell to the ground immediately, covering his face. Gradually he raised his eyes, feeling the intense heat emitted by the blast that had turned the soldier to charred ruins.

He raised himself from the ground and ordered his men to beat out the grass fire. Going over to the seared body of his man, he kicked the remains several times, cursing the ignorant peasants he was forced to serve and contend with. The fire was extinguished by the time his anger was vented on the burned and blackened corpse.

His trackers pointed the way, and he urged his men after their quarry. Night fell suddenly and completely. He cursed his luck. There was nothing darker than the jungle at night.

Moving south, according to his compass, Casey kept his people going for several more hours. Casey was tired as hell and knew that the others had to be also. He stopped for a brief interval to see how the women of his group were faring. In the darkness, he bumped into Yu Li. This time he did not back away. Neither did she.

"How are you doing? Do you need rest yet?" His voice was almost a whisper yet seemed loud in the jungle stillness.

"No," she whispered, "but soon my mother will."

Casey could read the concern in her voice for her mother. He liked that. There was nothing like the respect the Orientals held for their kin.

"Don't worry, little one. If we must, I'll have the men take turns carrying her. We will leave no one behind."

Yu Li drew herself erect, proudly determined. "Little one is what you call children. I am no child."

Her direct look and defiance made him swallow, half choking. He composed himself and chuckled.

"You're right there, Yu Li. You're certainly no child."

George turned the position of point man over to one of Phang's young Kamserai, giving him a few words of advice that the soldier promptly ignored. They moved on through the night, with brush and vines whipping at their faces and arms. You can't fight the jungle, Casey thought. You either move with it or wear yourself out. Flowing with the show, not fighting the land and its lay, they weaved and twisted, bent and crawled, until Casey finally called a halt to their march near a small stream.

"One hour," he told them all. "Sleep if you possibly can. I will take first watch on our back trail. Van, you take the front. Go out about fifty meters only. Come back in close as we start to move out."

Van nodded in agreement. Hoisting his HK G-3, he faded into the shadows and vanished quickly from their view.

Huan was comforting his wife, assuring her that their children were in good hands and safe. Yu Li headed for the stream to get them some water. No one had to tell the Cambodian mercenaries not to smoke or make noise. Phang had trained them well. Each of the men settled into his own private world and thoughts. Some went to sleep instantly, and others spent the time repairing rips in their clothing or mending damaged gear. A few ate cold balls of rice slowly, as exhausted men will do.

All of them had run hard that day. From the time of the first grenades up to now, none had slowed. The rest that any of them had enjoyed had been little.

Casey went back the way they had come. About fifty meters to their rear he sat down, his back resting against a tree. Removing his camouflage cap, he used it to wipe the sweat from his face. He took the lid off his canteen and took a long pull of the warm water. He rinsed his mouth, spat it out, took another, and swallowed. He poured some of the water into his hat, using it as a rag to wash his face and chest, enjoying its freshness. Though warm, the water cooled him as it mingled with the perspiration. His body gave a slight shiver as the liquid ran down the hairs of his chest and soaked the shirt at his waist. Wiping the back of his hand across his mouth, he settled into himself, trying to plan ahead.

Of all the damned luck, he thought. They'd almost made it. What were the damned Khmer troops doing in this area in the first place? Phang had told him there was no reason for them to be this far out. Their only mission could have been looking for us. Somehow they knew we were coming. How? Who gives a damn how? They had to get out. Get out. Get out or die; and it was a long way out if they didn't arrange a pickup some way or another and find some damned place away from here.

A small crackling sound, maybe a branch snapping beneath someone's weight, jerked Casey to instant alertness. The Swedish "K" he carried swung automatically around to the direction of the sound.

"It is me," came a small voice. "Yu Li." She approached him on her kees, her hands feeling the way through the darkness until she touched him.

"What is it, damn it?" he hissed. "What are you doing out here?"

"Hold your temper, big nose. I bring you food." Pulling herself alongside him, she handed him a cloth. Inside was rice and sardines, along with the ever-present *nuoc mam* sauce for spicing the food. He grunted in acceptance and ate, chewing slowly and noiselessly. She watched, waiting until he was finished and then placing the cloth back inside her clothing. She raised herself until her eyes were level with his. Casey thanked her for the food, smiling.

Yu Li spoke, her eyes unwavering: "I'm going to take good care of you. I will not have a man who is weak. You must eat and keep up your strength."

"What the hell do you mean by that?" Casey snapped in a whisper, starting to rise.

Yu Li's hands fell on his big shoulders, forcing him back to his seat. "Sh! Hold your voice down, big nose. I made up my mind when you first came to our cave. You would be my man, and I saw in your eyes that you wanted me also. Good! So be it. I will have you, and you shall have me."

Casey started to respond to her statement, but protest was impossible. Her mouth covered his, molding itself to his lips. A long sweet blending, her tongue sugary and serpentlike, slithering into his mouth, searching out its depths. He seemed to breath her in, his arms reaching to pull her to him, but she slipped from his arms easily.

"Not now, ugly one. Later!"

She faded back into the dark of the jungle, back to the rest area, leaving him there in a state of near shock. Damn, he thought. I feel like something has been pulled out of me. The little bitch means it. She wants me and means to have me. Shit! If that kiss was any indication of things to come, she might get her way.

Their hour of rest was over. He returned to the camp area, rounding them all up and counting. They moved to the south and arrived at the edge of a swamp at about dawn.

Casey waved Van over, and they approached Phang.

"Do you know this place," Casey asked the old man.

"I have been here before, Casey, but no man knows it very well. It runs for many miles in many directions."

"Can we hide in it?" Casey demanded.

"Oh, yes, young one. Many have hidden in these wetlands. Perhaps many still do."

Casey thought about it for a moment before speaking. He put his hand to his jaw pensively. "Phang, what do you think? Should we lay up here for a while? It looks to me like it may be a good place to lose those mothers behind us."

Phang agreed. "Yes, it would be hard for them to know which way we went in these swampy lands. Perhaps it would do us no harm at all to rest here and wait for night to cover us.''

The three of them turned, walking back to the others. Casey snapped his orders to them all, with Phang echoing the American's words in translation.

''Okay, everybody into the water. We'll go in for a mile or so, then cut over to the west and find a place to lay up for the night. We can all use the rest, and we should be safe.''

In Casey's opinion, Huan's wife seemed to have caught her second wind. She was moving fast and doing nicely, close beside her man. Huan was helping her whenever she faltered, smiling encouragement as they treaded through the water and slime of the swamp. Yu Li was close by Casey's side, grabbing his arm at times. He caught Huan's eye on him once, and Huan shrugged knowingly, as if to say, ''What can I do? You're a trapped man.'' Casey grinned back weakly.

George and Van were not slow to notice what was going on between him and the girl, and they deliberately let their conversation run to the proper care and beating of women. He chose to ignore their quips, knowing that to respond would only urge them on to greater efforts.

The going was relatively easy at first. Then the mud, black and stinking, began to build up on their feet. Great black lumps clung to them, growing ever heavier and more burdensome. The stench was from thousands of tiny plants, animals, and insects that had died, trapped in the mud to decay, the gases from their bodies forming small pockets by the thousands, breaking open and releasing their foul odors with every step of the invaders, filling their noses with the putrid smell of death and rot, releasing their odious contents to rest in the throats of the thoughtless and careless intruders in this land of no man.

About 1000 hours they located a hummock, raised from the ground level of the swampy fen. It seemed reasonably dry underfoot. Casey turned to them all, smiling.

''Okay, troops. This is the place. We camp here. Phang,

I think you can let your boys make some small fires and cook us a meal. Have them make enough to last through the night, too.''

"Very good, my son.''

Phang passed permission to build fires, and in less than a minute's time, small wisps of smoke were mingling with what seemed to be a permanent condition of low fog, hanging in the trees. Most of the trees had leaves and foliage only on their upper branches. What the Americans would call Spanish moss and the Spanish would call French moss hung in ghostlike strings from trees that resembled the cypresses found in the Florida everglades. A number of snakes found their way into the camp area, making their presence known to the intruders. To their immediate deteriment, they became a portion of the noon meal.

After their poor but sufficient feast, all of them spent a great deal of time scraping an unbelievable amount of mud from their footwear. Casey instructed George to have them all clean their weapons before resting and to make very sure that sentries were out and alert. He doubted that Phang's men would be slack in their duties, but it never hurt to double-check. The Khmer Rouge were not fools and possibly were already on their trail and closing fast.

CHAPTER FOURTEEN

Casey had no way of knowing how correct his thoughts were. Lon and his men were resting at the same spot where their prey had entered the waters of the swamp.

Souvang reported to his colonel. "Master, they have gone into the swamp. Do we follow?"

"Do we follow? Of course we follow, you fool! Do you think I have endured all we've gone through just to give up the hunt at this point? Do you honestly think I would chance losing them now? Get the men on their worthless feet!"

Lon's men entered the stagnant waters uneasily. Most of them, like Lon, were not born to the jungle. What lay in store for them must be learned by experiencing it. The old hands, the ones who'd been raised in these forsaken lands, could not have told them anything that would have given them the slightest comfort as far as these water were concerned. Bad, that's what the waters were. Bad!

But they feared the wrath of their commander more than what lay in wait ahead. They entered and followed him, with the Meo casting about for any signs of passage. It took some time, but even in this maze of mud and slime, the Meo followed the nearly invisible spoor of their prey.

A slight discoloration of the water, where small dead leaves and insects floated, showed that someone or something had passed this place or that. Another gave them direction, and they followed, slowly but surely, each clog-

ging step taking them ever closer. They followed, with
Lon relentless in his determination to overtake them.

Casey's party rested, holding their weapons to their
chests like spears even as they slept. Casey opened his
eyes to find his jungle boots sitting beside him, spotlessly
clean, with no trace of mud or slime. All of his other gear
had been treated, the same, right down to his holster. He'd
taken it off before falling asleep, content that the Swedish
"K" was propped on his belly, his hand on the grip, ready
for use.

Yu Li had proclaimed to all that he was hers. She knelt
before him now. Somehow, he noticed, she had managed
to clean herself. Even her nails were spotlessly clean.

"Eat," she said, holding a bowl of rice to his face. As
soon as he started to protest, she stuffed his mouth full of
rice. "Eat, big nose. Do not talk! Eat and keep up your
strength."

Casey sputtered and swallowed. "All right, damn it to
hell!" he bellowed in a low voice, "maybe you're right.
But even if you are, I am the boss. You will do as I say, or
I'll turn you over my knee and spank that pretty little ass
of yours until it looks like sunset. Do you understand me,
woman?"

Yu Li bowed her head, looking pleased at his outburst.
"Yes, I understand. You are the master. I am sorry if I
have offended you. If you wish, you may beat me now."

Casey grunted, confused by her quick acceptance of his
demands. "No, not right now. But go and fetch Phang.
Bring him to me."

"Yes, my master." Yu Li bowed deeply and left him.

Huan watched them until his daughter had left. He
approached the American who'd come to save them.

"Ah, my young friend, it is indeed serious. Never have
I seen her submit to anyone or anything. You are in a lot
of trouble. A word of wisdom from one who has much
experience with this she-devil child. The next time she
offers for you to beat her, do it. You will understand why I
tell you this afterward." Huan left him there, a father

shaking his head in sympathy for the man who had gained his daughter's affection.

Why in the hell, Casey thought, couldn't they all mind their own damned business? They were all turning this into a thing he didn't want to happen. Yet it was happening. He could feel it, not only in his loins but in his heart. And it was no damned good, especially for her. He remembered the others he'd loved, the ones who had found affection for Casca, and he for them. He'd loved them all. He'd outlived them all, and he'd lost them all to a thing called time. Time was something that he'd always had plenty of, but it was a bastardly thing that they couldn't share, and it was no use to pretend that it would be any different this time. Phang knelt beside him, bringing him out of his reverie.

"Yes, young lover of Chinese girls, what is it you bade of me? My wisdom in the handling of women perhaps?"

"Knock that crap off, Phang, you old degenerate. The question is this: How do we get out of this damned place?"

Phang pointed slowly to the west and then moved his hand in the direction of the east. "Take your pick, young one."

Casey pointed to the west. "At least we'll be out of this hummock for awhile. Farther west will put us closer to the vector of the aircraft when it returns." He rose, stretching.

Once more, they all took their individual positions for the march and snaked their way through the cypresslike trees. All day they marched, waging war with the uncountable swarms of insects. Mosquitoes and jungle ticks were doing their best to devour them. Phang and his men doused themselves liberally with repellent from their survival kits. Casey gave his repellent to Yu Li, since her eyes were asking why the insects refused to bite him. The act of their avoiding him puzzled her greatly but only reminded Casca—or Casey. Sometimes he forgot about the time he'd been tied to the tidal stakes at Helsfjord in northern Scandinavia. He grinned now, remembering how the crabs had slithered sideways, nipping at his legs and just as quickly moving off, refusing to taste further. Even the fish and a cruising shark drawn by the blood caused by the crab bites had refused to make a meal of him. Flesh and blood cursed by the Jew, Jesus, at Golgotha was evidently not worth feeding on. And so it was with the mosquitoes and ticks here today.

He commented to Yu Li and the others who'd noticed it that he was too mean to bite; his skin was too tough to penetrate. None of them had been convinced, he thought.

Van and George shared their repellent with Yu Li's parents. The hours passed, and then, between the trees, rising like a mirage, covered with vines and ground growth, a tiered temple, of the kind built by Khmer kings six hundred years ago, found at Angor Wat, suddenly loomed ahead. This one was old, showing centuries of neglect.

The Kamserai were silent as they approached the temple. The ground fog swirled around it, rising higher. There was no fog on the ground now; it hung above their heads thirty or forty feet, like a cloud, obscuring the sky from their view. Unless one had a watch on his arm, Casey thought, it would be impossible to tell whether it was night or day.

"Okay," he yelled. "We rest here for a while. Van, take a couple of Phang's men and check out the building. The rest of you find positions and take a break. No fires," he added, "but you can smoke." Phang made the translation to the rest, adding a few orders of his own.

A temple, Casey reckoned. He'd heard many stories and read of people finding things like this. He wished he had a camera. Yu Li came beside him, putting her small hand in his. Casey froze for a moment. If he rejected her now, there would only be the immediate pain to suffer. He couldn't find the strength to do it. Slowly, his fingers closed lightly around hers. An agreement was reached between them without a word being spoken. Yu Li was his woman now, and all knew it. He knew that he would live to regret it.

Van reported back that the interior of the temple was

clear and uninhabited except for the usual guests: bats and rats. Some of the rats, Van said laughingly, were so huge that their cocks touched the ground, leaving five tracks everywhere they ran. Casey wasn't amused. He remembered some prior encounters with the dirty rodent bastards.

"Okay," he ordered, "you can build a fire inside. Start the Kamserai to cooking. Phang, you keep a guard mounted. We will rest here for a while."

He took Yu Li by the hand again, entering the darker shadows of the temple. A feeling of heavy quiet settled on them, with all wondering if they were the first to enter this sanctum in hundreds of years. Brushing aside cobwebs, they entered the larger inner chamber, past walls intricately carved with shadowy figures, dust and time obscuring them so that he could not make out exactly what they were or what they were supposed to be doing. He'd check them out closer a little later, when he had the time, after brushing them off for a better look.

Arriving in what must have been considered the principal room of the temple, Casey chose a spot near the southern corner and dropped his gear. Yu Li began immediately to clear and clean the area, preparing to cook for him. He sighed defeatedly. I'm sunk, he thought. She's got me for sure now. Shaking his head in resignation, he left to check on the others.

Van had taken up position above them, where he could see out and into the clearing that any intruder would have to cross to get to the temple. Casey considered it a damned good observation area and waved to Van, agreeing with his choice. The clearing, he thought, must at one time have been set with flat stones. Trees were growing, but only a few, and only in certain spots, as if they'd been planted for the purpose of providing courtyard shade. A few stones could also be seen here and there, twisted from their original positions by the growths, pushing their way upward between the paving stones.

Van was almost high enough to touch the ceilinglike fog

over his head. But the sky was still not to be seen. Casey
watched as he settled himself, checked his G-3, and set it
across his lap. He took one deep breath, sighed heavily,
and fell asleep before the sigh had been completed.

He grinned and went to check on George. He found him
trying to interest the other Cambodians in a Montagnard
gambling game that George was an expert at. But the
Cambodian mercenaries were apparently wise to him by
now and would have no part of it.

When Casey was sure that all was in order outside, he
returned to the temple. He wanted to check out the carv-
ings a little closer before it was time to eat.

Lon's lead troops had just reached the hummock of
ground that Casey and his crew had vacated a couple of
hours before. His Meo scout quickly informed him that
they were not far behind now. Lon had slipped, losing his
footing while climbing up and onto the bank of the hummock. Now he was sitting and having his boots cleaned of
the mud and slime by one of his men. He digested the
input of the Meo tracker while he ate. He called in his
squad leaders.

"They are close ahead," he told them. "Silence is the
order of the day until I say otherwise. Woe unto anyone
who fails to obey this command. You would all do well to
remember the young fool who needed the cigarette so badly
that it was worth his life."

His squad leaders gulped at the memory, still fresh in
their minds, remembering how the young trooper's eyes
had tried to jump from their sockets as he was strangled.

Lon donned his boots when the soldier had finished. He
gathered his troops. With the Meo leading the way, Lon
once again headed them all down the trail of whatever lay
ahead. It irked him not to know who they were or what
they'd come for. But the fact that they were here was
enough to serve his purpose. That they were unaware of
how close he was was gravy on the rice. The Meo trackers
were his secret weapon. He'd have them in custody before
too much longer.

Shortly before nightfall, his point scout, the Meo he had threatened, came running to him, pointing ahead.

"They are in a ghost house just ahead. They are here. I have seen them with my eyes, great one."

Lon started to run ahead of his men. Then suddenly he checked himself. There was no use rushing things at this stage of the game, he thought. He had to get hold of himself.

Calling his leaders to his side, he put them into a skirmishing line, reinforcing his edict of silence; telling his scouts to take a squad and circle wide of the enemy's location to cut off any attempt at retreat. He and the others would wait ten minutes before advancing.

The minutes dragged by. The adrenal glands began to increase their output, which manifested itself in an increased heartbeat, causing heavy sweating beneath his armpits, already streaked white from the loss of body salt.

It was time! The line advanced, weapons at the ready but fingers off the trigger. All of them were well aware of their fate should they fire a shot accidentally, warning their quarry of the advance.

They made their way slowly, cautiously, through the trees and undergrowth. The fog, hovering over them like an ominous cloud of death, didn't make them feel any better. The Meo's words a short time before, telling their commander that the foreigners were in a ghost house, had stirred superstitions that lay just beneath their conscious minds, and had brought them easily to the surface.

They all crept deftly closer. All eyes were on the lead Meo as he suddenly raised himself to an erect position, throwing his hands into the air. Wordlessly, he did not halt in that position for long. Instead, as if in slow motion, he fell straight backward to the ground. One of the Khmer Rouge ran quickly to see why he had fallen. As he reached the Meo, a small dot appeared in the center of his forehead and a much larger hole opened up the back of his skull, allowing approximately thirty percent of his gray matter to exit with the burst. He too dropped silently to the soft plushness of the ground.

Still there were no sounds. The Khmer troops hit the ground and froze, eyes wide with fear. Death, silent death, was reaching out and striking them noiselessly. Could it be the spirits from the ghost house?

CHAPTER FIFTEEN

Whispered word of their arrival had reached Casey's ears inside. He moved quickly to the area below Van's position outside. Van's words were barely audible over the natural sounds of the jungle night.

"Khmer Rouge! They are here. I just took two of them out. The reason they have been able to stay with us so easily is that they have at least one Meo scout. Correction, make that had one Meo scout. I just wasted him and also one Khmer with the use of my silencer. For the time being, I suppose they are confused. But that won't last for long."

Casey nodded and motioned for him to stay put. Back inside, he gathered his gear and headed for the door, telling Phang to get his troops in position and ready. Hoisting the MG-34, he stood behind a column and fed a belt of ammo into the gun. He pulled the cocking lever and waited. Moving his head, peering around the ancient pillar, he ran his eyes over the trees at the edge of the clearing.

"Okay," he whispered to all within earshot. "They're out there. Don't waste ammo. Let's see what we're up against first. Phang."

Evidently the old man hadn't heard him. Casey whispered a little louder this time. "Phang!" He saw a nod of acknowledgment . "You and your men lay back for a little bit. No use in giving away our numbers. George, Van, selec-

tive fire. We don't want to let them know we have automatic fire until we really need it. Use full auto only if they
rush us. Got it?''

Each of them nodded. Lying down on his belly, Casey
put the MG on selective fire, spread out the bipods on the
weapon, and settled down behind it.

Phang looked at the scarred monstrous torso of his
friend Casey Romain, lying determined and deadly-looking
behind the machine gun. He was a leader, all right, and a
good one. He wondered how eyes like Casey's, filled with
grit and resolution of action ahead, could at other times
hold so much love for men such as Phang himself or for a
small Chinese girl. Those eyes, Phang reckoned, had seen
more of everything, including hate and love, than their
owner cared to admit. He loved this American or whatever
he was. They would all make it through the night if only
because of this man, Casey Romain. He thought he saw
movement by the trees then, and he turned back to other
observations, reminding himself to one day talk more with
this man. Maybe he would learn something about him
other than the fact that he was a warrior and could be
trusted.

Lon started to move to the area where two of his men,
including the Meo scout, had fallen. But he thought better
of it. Obviously, it was a dangerous place to be right now.
Dropping behind one of the trees, he wondered what it
could be. He had hardly finished the thought when a
crease appeared on the side of the tree covering him,
throwing splinters in his face. He fell to his belly. Silencer! That's what it is. They have a sniper with a silencer on
his weapon. No matter if we make noise or not now. They
know we are here.

Lon yelled for his men to take cover. It was a useless
gesture of command. His men were biting the soil, wish-
ing they could get even deeper. Then he talked to them
quietly and reassuringly, telling them that the enemy had a
silenced rifle. That was what had killed the Meo and their

comrade in arms. There was no need to worry or fear the unknown.

Slowly they raised their heads, looking at the clearing. They'd been foolish to believe in spirits. One by one they edged along on their elbows and stomachs until they reached the clearing. Their bellies quickly became soaked with moisture from the ground, which was covered carpetlike with a combination of short grass and moss. They wormed their way forward.

Casey let his eyes wander, thinking, Aha, there's one. They were edging their way up to the clearing; best to keep them from getting too close. He let his weapon settle on the figure lying in the short grass close to the base of one of the trees. He could just make out the outline of his face.

He aimed, estimating the distance at one hundred twenty yards. Taking a deep breath, assuring himself that the man's face was sitting perfectly atop the sight, he released half of what he'd inhaled and slowly squeezed the trigger.

The gun bucked once, riding almost straight back into his shoulder. The 7.62-mm round entered the Khmer's face just below the upper lip, blowing off his lower jaw and ripping its way lengthwise through the chest to explode the lungs. It continued on its deadly course, into the abdominal cavity, finally exiting just above the man's left hip. Inside, the man was left a mass of black jelly from the bullet's passage. The slug had set up shock waves in front of it as it passed through, building up pressure until everything in or near its path was smashed. When the bullet exited the man's body, it was twisted and flattened but flew on for another thirty feet before bouncing off a tree. There was not sufficient power left to penetrate the bark.

Three down, Casey thought. Van got two, and I got one. That should put then on slow for a while.

A burst of automatic fire came ripping back at him from the treeline. Like fireflies, the gun flashes winked at him from the short distance. Chips were blown off the old temple's columns and the aged walls behind him, falling here and there. Oh ho, he thought. I got into their shit that time. He heard a quick command in Cambode tongue barked from the trees beyond the clearing. The firing stopped. Well, well! So that's what their boss sounds like?

Casey waved to his two comrades and his old friend Phang. Together they crept back into the interior of the temple for a short and quiet meeting. Phang's Kamserai had been placed in position to take over for the men inside. Casey noticed that Huan had taken the Swedish "K" and had placed himself on watch between the open doorway and his wife and daughter.

"Phang, send one of your boys to scout the insides of this place. See if there are any exits we haven't found, ones that the Khmer Rouge could possibly find to get in before we could get out."

Phang gave a short command from the doorway, and the same man who had set the grenades in position on the trail left his post and came inside, heading back into the unexplored section of the old building.

Casey turned to Phang once again. "What do you think, wise one?"

It was Phang's turn to smile. "Oh, so now it's the wise one, is it? Before, I was what you called a degenerate, I believe. But no matter, as I have often heard you say, my son. This time we are in a world of shit."

Casey turned to Van. "Van, do you have any suggestions?"

Van shook his head. "Not right at the present, I'm afraid."

George, too, shook his sweaty noggin. Casey shrugged.

"Okay, gentlemen. Then we wait. The next move is up to our friends outside. One thing we do know is how they were able to follow us. Those Meos are some of the best trackers in the world. I worked with them a short time in 1963, back in Laos. What surprises me is the fact that they are working with the commies. But they are damned good, no matter which side they're working for." He turned, throwing up his hands. "If we can get out of here, we'll probably have a good chance of throwing the bastards off our trail. Van has taken the Meo out. Let's hope they had only one. But regardless, for the time being, everyone on watch. Right? They may try to rush us. So far we hold the upper hand, merely due to our position. Let's play it loose and watch the suckers for a while."

They returned to their individual positions outside the temple, each going through his own special and private preparations for combat. For some, it was prayer; for others, just getting their mental attitudes ready, psyching themselves.

A voice called to them from the treeline, this time in English, clear but with a slight accent.

"American? Do you hear me, American?" Lon's voice was loud. Casey grinned. That's my boy, the same voice he'd heard earlier. Their leader, no doubt. He knew there was an American involved. How? Someone had informed on them. Who? Ling. He would bet his ass that it was that bastard Ling.

"Yeah, I hear you," he called back. "What do you want?"

Lon grinned this time. Good, he thought. Now perhaps we can lure the rat from his hole. He cleared his throat before speaking.

"American, I am the military governor of this district. If you and your men will surrender, no one will be hurt. We are aware that you have women in your party; signs on the trail told us that. They will not be harmed, I assure you. I want only you and the other foreign invaders of our peaceful land. I knew many Americans in Phnom Penh years ago. Americans always protect their women. I, too, am a protector of women. So therefore, if they are harmed in any manner, it can only be considered your own fault, your responsibility. Think about it, American. You have one hour. My men have the temple surrounded. There is no escape; and you are outnumbered at least seven to one. Remember, only one hour!"

Well, well, Casey figured. So that's how many men he has. Seven to one. Not good for sure; but not as bad as it could have been. These Kamserai of Phang's are worth two of his men any time in a fair fight. That reduces the odds a little bit at least. Taking a breath, he called back to Lon.

"Okay, I hear you, Governor. We'll think over your offer. You're right. I don't want the women harmed in any way. Call back on us in an hour."

They could use the time, he thought. Slithering back into the temple, along with his men and Phang, he warned them.

"Keep on the alert. I not only don't trust that bastard, I don't like his smooth tongue, either. He's trying all the tricks. They may try to rush us while our guard is down for the hour, so let's don't let it down. We need to get them to try and rush us, though, at least before the night is out. His men have to be tired and hungry by now. We haven't stopped long, so it's for damned sure they couldn't have. If we get them to charge us, the automatic firepower of Van's G-3 and my MG should make a hell of a dent in their numbers; at least slow them up till morning."

He turned to the Kamserai chief. "Phang, any news from your man that's been checking out the rear of the interior yet?"

Phang shook his head. "No, nothing yet. It will be soon."

"Okay! Yu Li, you and your mother fix some chow. Check our water supply. I wouldn't want to drink that swamp stuff if we can possibly avoid it. Everybody take it easy but keep your ears and eyes open."

Yu Li came to his side. She knelt down and laid her head on his shoulder. In a small voice, she asked, "Is it bad?"

"Bad enough! I thought we had lost them. The leader of those men out there knows what he is doing to have stayed on our trail this long. I don't want to make the mistake of underestimating him. We just have to wait and see what comes down.''

Putting his arm around her shoulders, he hugged her. ''Yu Li, you go help your mother and get the medic kits out of all our bags. We'll probably need them before this is all over.'' He patted her on the butt. ''Scat, woman.''

George waited, apparently unconcerned by all that had transpired. From the vantage point he'd selected near the entrance, he let his eyes move across the ground in front of him, resting his shotgun over his knees. As his eyes wandered, so did his mind. George? he thought. A strange name for one like me. But it sounds more familiar to me now than does my real name. Trung Si, or Casey, as Van called him, had started to call him George after they had worked together for several months. Probably because he'd never been able to get his given name right. George instead of Cheo Rawge. The trail he had traveled with Casey and Van had been a good one, and if it had to end here, so be it. What difference did it make where or when one died as long as one did it well? I have seen enough killing in my time that the thought of my own death does not excite me. Long years I have spent fighting in one place or another. For the *Doum Broun* (the French long noses) I fought before I had all my body hair. I was young then. By their reckoning they figured I was thirteen to fifteen years old. I couldn't have known actually. We people of the Bihar do not have calendars like all others. Neither do we care if a certain day comes or goes. It is enough for us that we are.

The French had treated the people of the mountains as men. The French! He had not thought of them for some time, that was certain. That was when he'd started to become fond of big noses. Yes, they had treated us as men, not *moi* (animals), as did the Viets from the cities. We worked for the French because it gave us the opportunity to kill Viets and not be punished for doing so. Legionnaires. *Vive le Legion Étrange!* Three years with them. Strange men, those. They were never the same. The offi-

cers were French, the sergeants German, troopers . . .
now, they'd been everything, North Africans, Sudanese,
blacker than shoe polish, a few Italians, not many. And we
of the mountains, who served with the Indigene.

George smiled inside, remembering the good things of
his past: the drinking bouts, where the Germans always
seemed to win. They had also taught him many of their
great marching songs, though the words had been changed
to fit this new war they were fighting instead of the big
one in Europe. The Germans had proved to be good
comrades, as had all the men of the legion. They'd taught
him to speak their language, first the French, then the
Germans, and had shown him many things from a world
he hadn't even dreamed of. Nothing, before they'd come,
had existed outside his small village along the Dap Rao
River.

Letting a breath hiss from between his teeth, he sighed.
It was gone now, all gone. Some still lived, he supposed,
but most were dead. Dien Bien Phu, de Castrie, General
Giap of the Vietminh, Strong Point Monique, the surgeon,
a fine man who'd treated him for a shrapnel wound in the
thigh. What of him? Did he still live? George hoped so.

Those had been long days at Dien Bien Phu. Why they
had built there had always puzzled him. The ground was
no good; you couldn't build a decent bunker. As soon as it
rained, its sides would start caving in. Too much sand in
the ground. One spent more time worrying about being
buried alive in case of a near miss by one of the Viets'
105s than he did about being shot. One thing about the
legion, though—they treated everyone the same. They
were all soldiers of France, and no preference was given
because you were a Montagnard, a Viet, or even a German,
who had fought and conquered their country. To the French,
as long as you served France, you were French.

He recalled sadly the day of the surrender. That day,
Captain Fremont, the commander of George's unit, was
one of the few who had decided to break out rather than
surrender to the Vietminh. Of the twenty men of their unit

who'd broken free from their encirclement that night, only four had made it to the French lines. The remaining ten thousand men of Dien had been marched off to holding pens farther north to wait until peace came.

George, along with many others, had cried when the tricolored flag of France was taken down and the gold star of the communists was raised to take its place over Hanoi.

To stay in the north was impossible. George had moved south, along with almost a million others, to escape the rule of the Vietminh. He'd returned to his tribal home outside Pleiku in the central highlands of South Vietnam. There he'd waited, not knowing for what. Then the troubles had started again. An ambush here, a terror bombing there, assassinations and threats. The communists were not content with their lands to the north. No, like pigs, they wanted it all.

George, because of his background, was made a company commander of a unit of the CIDG, a self-defense force established throughout Vietnam. That had been his duty when he'd first met Casey and Van. Selections were being made for a spec unit, called a "mike force," consisting of specially trained Montagnards, Viets, and Americans, to conduct swift reaction raids on the Cong by chopper and parachute.

Again, because of George's knowledge and past history, he was made the native commander of the troops in the mike force. They had made many successful strikes against the Cong in those days. George knew the depth of Casey's feelings when they'd raided that village in Cambodia and had found out what happened to an American there. George had agreed completely with Casey's actions in making the Cong crawl by the dead American's grave on their stomachs. If George had had his own way that day, he personally would have killed them all and buried them in a mass grave at the dead American's feet so that he would have had no shortage of slaves in the next life. With that many slaves, he would certainly have been considered a chieftain. Contact with the west had not changed George's beliefs and his way of thinking. Many of the old ways still made more sense to him than the things he'd been taught and told by the *Doum Broun*, or big noses.

It wasn't until much later that George had learned that Casey had also been at Dien Bien Phu.

George was still deep in thoughts, both pleasant and unpleasant, when Lon's voice broke the silence of the night. The man's voice grated on George's ears, sending chills of remembrance and offensive shivers up and down his spine: memories of a voice that sounded a lot like this one some years before.

CHAPTER SIXTEEN

Lon called his sharpshooter to him, whispering. "Watch for the American's response. If it is negative to my question, your signal to fire will be the words, 'It is your choice, American.' Do you understand me?" His man nodded.

Lon yelled firmly and loud, his voice almost a shriek. "American, do you hear me? Your hour is up! What is your answer?" There was no response. "Come now, American, what is your answer? My decision will not be delayed. Answer me now or we attack and everyone dies. Men and women, do you hear?"

He whispered again to his rifleman. "If he exposes himself and we shoot him, the others should not be too difficult to deal with. The loss of the leader, the loss of the nerve."

"Answer me, American, you have no more time."

There was nothing in the night except the sound of his own voice.

Casey made his way back to the entrance of the temple, sliding outside to the same post he had lain behind an hour previous. Catching George's eye, he spoke in German. *"Bewacht!"* It was the German word for "beware."

George grunted. Did Trung Si think this was his first time out?

"Okay, Governor, we hear you. I need some more time to think it over."

Colonel Lon could just make out the shape of Casey's head behind the column. "What did you say, American? I did not hear you well."

Casey raised his head a little and repeated his request for more time.

When he moved, Lon spoke. "It is your choice, American."

Lon's man sighted. He fired with the last word from his colonel's mouth. The bullet burned a path less than an inch from Casey's face, making the unmistakable sound of a single clap, meaning you'd almost taken one—the round had broken the wind by your ear. Casey felt the familiar twinge of cold fear pass through his gut, and his ass tightened with what was clinically known as tenesmus, or the spasmodic tensing of the anal muscles.

Pulling himself lower, he called out, "All right, you yellow asshole, you called the game. It's up to you how we play it now." With his last words, he moved to the opposite side of the column and called inside to Phang. "Get your people ready. I think we'll be hit soon. Any word from your man in the rear?"

"None yet," called the old one, "but he must have found something to be taking so long."

"Damnit, go and check him out. We can't wait all night."

The old Kamserai gave a few quick instructions to his men and disappeared into the darkness at the rear of the temple. Making his way around falling and crumbled stone and dank, musty growth, he went the way his man had gone before him, stooping and crawling in places where the roof of one room had partially collapsed. No light was visible through the hole in the ceiling. Taking his flashlight out, he snapped the beam on full and made his way deeper into the rear of the temple.

The beam of his torch picked up the feet and lower legs of his man, protruding from a hole barely large enough for a good-sized man to crawl through. Phang went to him, kicking the bottom of his feet.

"What is wrong with you, lazy one? Are you asleep?"

The answer to his question came with a lightning swift streak that threw itself at Phang's face, barely missing as the old man leaped backward. A giant tree cobra had lunged, striking at its prey and missing by only millimeters. Several drops of golden venom fell to the floor as the serpent's hollow fangs overfilled and leaked with the expectation of another kill. It lay unmoving for only seconds.

The giant serpent pulled itself forward, toward Phang, curling, coiling, raising its head to a height that was level with the old man's eyes. Their organs of sight locked.

Phang started to take a step to his rear and felt a cool stone touch his hip. No way to escape here. The giant cobra moved slowly forward as if aware that his quarry had no place to run. No escape route. An easy victim waited.

Phang stopped all motion, locking his eyes again on the snake's. The cobra hissed, letting its split tongue dart in and out, tasting the air about it, sensing the heat of the prey before it.

Phang began to rock slowly from side to side, as he'd seen old women of the snake cults do. Gradually increasing his motions from side to side, he continued rocking. The ancient serpent began to ape his movements, its eyes never leaving Phang's—lidless, unblinking eyes, yellow with untold years.

Options passed through Phang's mind. He could not keep moving like this forever, and if his attention left the snake for even an instant, he would die. No time to call for help. Even if they heard him, there would be no time. He must do it, whatever there was that could be done, himself. So be it! The time to move was now.

Increasing the reach of his sway, Phang without hesitation threw his left hand suddenly to the side. The cobra, in rapt attention, went instinctively for the object in motion. In less time than the blink of an eye, the serpent's fangs sank deeply into his hand, catching his palm in the center. At the strike, Phang's fist closed around the cobra's head, keeping the deadly fangs embedded in the palm. In one clean, swift motion, he pulled his long razor-sharp blade from the scabbard on his right side and, in a continuous swing, severed the head of the snake from its body. He swung once more, even before the severed trunk of the cobra could hit the floor, and felt a cold and then a burning pain as the blade in his right hand cleaved his left hand at the wrist, allowing the fist, still locked tightly on the head of the cobra, to fall to the floor, joining the divided body that lay there as if it were still alive; writhing, moving as if it possessed a separate brain from the one Phang's clenched fist still held.

He dropped the blade, grabbing his left arm at the wrist and squeezing tightly to arrest the flow of blood. He squatted down, holding his arm in close, and waited to see whether he'd been swift enough to beat the venom's race to the circulatory track. A few seconds more and he would live or die.

It was hard to tell for sure. Was the burning in his mutilated arm from the poison or from his own quick amputation? Rocking back and forth on his heels, still squatting, he closed his eyes, taking quick, shallow breaths. The seconds passed. Rising, he looked down at the still writhing, winding body of the giant cobra. He knew that he had beaten the venom.

"Well, old one, we are even. You took one of my men and my hand. I will leave you both and forgive you. This was your home for decades. We were the intruders. You were only protecting your domain. Keep my hand and my man. Perhaps one or the other will serve you in the next incarnation. Peace, old one!"

Phang released his arm long enough to pull the body of his Kamserai warrior from the hole. Bending, he examined the entrance. It was not far! He could see a brighter glow about fifty feet away, filtering in from the outside. Perhaps this would prove to be their way out. Pushing and crawling, holding his bleeding and tender stump close to his chest and out of the way, he inched through the hole and across the space until the light was clear enough to show a partially covered exit. Looking out carefully, he could see that the wall of the treeline came right up to the opening. The swamp was just outside. Not much would have to be done to clear enough rocks away to be able to get out. The tunnel he was in appeared to have been an old drainage ditch, a shaft to release the waters during the rainy season.

Phang withdrew and returned to the main chamber. His arm was throbbing, but he would bear the pain. Men of his race prided themselves on their ability to endure anguish that would drive western men insane. He'd been gone no more than ten minutes, when he entered the main chamber and fell at Casey's feet. He smiled, looking up at Casey's questioning eyes.

"We have a way out, my son." He closed his eyes and fell into deep slumber.

Casey threw his arms up in wonderment. "What the hell are you doing sleeping now? Those bastards outside aren't going to wait much longer before rushing—"

He was interrupted. A gush of bright red arterial blood spurted out and into the dirt. He stared at the raw bleeding stump of Phang's arm and caught it before it could fall into the dirt beside him. Taking time for no more inquiries, he squeezed tightly, reaching into his first-aid kit with his other hand. He removed a roll of gauze bandages and quickly bound the severed wrist of his friend. Time for questions later. But what had he said before passing out? A way out?

The day was beginning to gnaw on Casey's nerves. But now, with the message of a way out from his placid old friend, things were looking somewhat better. He left Phang to the care of Yu Li and her mother and returned to the doorway, smiling at Huan, who was still vigilant and protective of his brood. Taking his old .34, keeping the piece on single shot, he pulled back inside to where the shadows covered him. Full night would be on them soon. That, combined with the dense, impenetrable fog overhead, would give them additional cover. But it would also make it more difficult to see one's target. If it was going to happen, it would be soon.

"Van," he called. "George. Get ready and stay close to me. When I pull out, don't linger. Phang says there's a way out of here in the rear. Keep close when I say so."

Receiving affirmative responses from both men, he lay down behind the gun and waited, placing himself slightly off to one side so that he couldn't be hit by any direct fire coming in from the entrance and could still cover the doorway with his weapon. He hoped Phang's men were ready. How would they react under fire without their chief? he wondered.

Lon gathered his men around him, whispering orders. "Attack! We attack now! We have them outnumbered seven to one. Give them to me, and I promise each of you shall be rewarded. Fail me, and you shall all pay dearly, directly to me personally. It appears that they have only a couple of submachine guns. Move rapidly and show no mercy. These are our enemies and would destroy us and our nation."

For this attack, there would be no fancy battle plans. A straight assault, head on at the enemy, using superior numbers to win would be his only tactic. There was no way out from the rear, according to his scouts, and with luck a few survivors of this slaughter would give him sufficient information to allow him to gain in stature at central headquarters.

Dull and heavy, the repeated sound of 60-mm mortars striking the temple signaled the attack from the Khmer Rouge. The mortars, however, were having little effect on the stone walls and ceiling of the old temple other than stirring up dust that made it hard to breathe.

Van yelled down. "Here they come!" Automatic fire and screams from the attacking Khmer made it sound as if an entire division was trying to reduce this one small stronghold.

They came, weapons firing. Van switched his piece to auto fire and, taking careful aim at the oncoming enemy, reduced their numbers by twos and threes each time the HK G-3 cut loose. A group of four Khmer soldiers reached the right side of the temple and were working their way along the columns leading to the entrance when George rose from his position.

Raising his automatic shotgun to hip level, he slowly squeezed the trigger. The combination of the bore's contents—buckshot and solid rounds—ripped through the backs of the stunned Khmer troops, the lead tearing holes in their bodies large enough for a grown man to stand in with his boots on, shredding their clothing to rags.

Leaping over the dead Khmers, George raced inside and lay down beside Casey, who was in the process of reloading. Van followed close behind and took up position on the opposite side of the doorway.

The Khmer rushed them in a rage at the loss of their comrades. They threw themselves into the doorway of the temple, firing blindly, confident that their numbers would give them victory, as their commander had said. They raced to meet death at this disputed barricade.

Casey cut loose on full automatic, letting his piece take command. Six hundred plus rounds per minute, ten per second, poured from the barrel, ripping their way through the massed bodies of the Khmer soldiers packed into the entrance of the temple. He hosed them down, supported by Van's G-3 and George's shotgun. The Kamserai were doing their best to reduce the odds also. Motioning for the soldiers of Phang to retreat while he and his two men covered them, Casey yelled for them to take Phang and head for the rear of the temple in order to cover them when they broke contact with the Khmer.

Suddenly, the assault from the Khmer ceased. They were taking up stations outside the doorway, several of them crawling up the porticoes to see whether there was any way in from the top. Realizing their new strategy, Casey and his men moved quickly to the next chamber to their rear, deciding to defend one room at a time as they retreated. The interior of the temple was almost pitch black. They rested for the next onslaught. Casey reloaded, knowing that his men were doing the same.

There was no immediate attack coming now, and he decided to use the break to check out Phang's exit. He wondered then how old Phang was faring. If they didn't get him something to prevent infection soon, he would die. He told George to take over the MG. Flipping his flash-light from his belt, he headed for the rear, passing Yu Li and her family on the way. The Kamserai were also in position two rooms behind Van and George's location. Phang was being looked after by two of his men.

Casey moved as fast as he could in the darkness of the interior, waving his flashlight here and there, seeing where Phang and his men had left tracks in the floor's aged dust. Following this trail, he weaved and half crawled until he came upon the body of Phang's man. He saw the remains of the giant serpent and Phang's hand still holding onto its head. He knew then what had happened previously and felt even more respect for the old man. It had taken a lot of courage for the old man to lop off his own hand. It was damned painful. As he looked down at the hand, Casey remembered the time he'd lost his own, at Kushan, or Afghanistan. He'd been ready to leave Persia, heading for China. The elder, Dacort, had chopped it off because—ah, hell, that was too many terrible years ago. At least he'd gotten his back. Phang never would. What kind of warrior could he be with one hand?

He bent down, peering through the hole in the wall. Looking in, he saw the small tunnel Phang had passed through. This had to be the way out that he'd mentioned. Putting himself into the passage, he followed it to its end. He studied it for only moments before deciding, like Phang, that this was their way out.

Tearing out the blocking stones and growths of centuries past, he stuck his head out into the night, breathing deeply of the cooler air, fresh compared with the stale air of the tube he'd just passed through.

Drawing back, he reentered the chamber he'd just left

and went directly to Yu Li. Somehow he'd almost forgotten that her father, Huan, was in charge of the family. Now that she was his woman, it seemed natural that she should be second in command. He'd change that outside. He didn't wish to offend her old man. That was easy to do with Orientals.

"We've found our ticket out of this hellhole." He could see she hadn't understood the use of "ticket." He broke it all down in somewhat better English, telling her what they must do.

Yu Li had moved back to care for Phang, and Casey could see that he was starting to come around. He said aloud to the girl, "God, he's a tough old bird." He looked down at Phang, speaking softly. "How are you, my father?"

"Your father? Is that what it is now? I am so desperate that I must have a big-nosed, round-eye for a son? Ha. Your father! May Buddha and all the holy ones have mercy on me if that sad condition is true."

Casey chuckled. "Yeah, I see you're all right, you old bastard. You're too mean to die."

Phang grunted. "That's better. Now I know you. You're Casey Romain. The one with little respect."

"I found your hand, Phang. Do you want it?"

"No." He sighed. "It belongs to the snake now. Leave it to him."

"Good enough," Casey replied. "I found your exit. Are you well enough to travel?"

Phang nodded. "If I am not, leave me here."

"Not on your life, old man, and I mean that. We came together, and while there's a chance for any of us, we leave together. In the meantime, eat these." He handed Phang four tetracycline tablets from his first-aid kit and gave the bottle containing the rest to Yu Li. "Give him two of these every four hours until there are no more."

Leaving Yu Li to tend to Phang, he returned to Van and George, informing them of the opening that Phang had found.

"We will try and hold them here at this door until later

in the night. Then, when they seem to have settled down, we will leave quietly. I think we'll be able to hold them for a while. So far, we've hurt them pretty bad while losing none of our own. There's only one way in, so periodically toss a couple of rounds in their direction to keep their heads down.''

George nodded and fired two great thumping shots down the narrow hallway. The echo, bouncing off the chamber walls, made it sound like a small cannon had just gone off.

''That should keep them down for a time, Trung Si.'' He rolled over and fell asleep after telling Van to take watch. George never failed to amaze Casey, or Van either for that matter. The bastards could sleep anywhere under any condition.

Right now, he thought, it looks like a Mexican standoff. They're out there, and we're in here. There's only one way in for them, and they think there's only one way out for us. I've got news for the commie bastards. If they'll refrain from attacking before dawn, there won't be a damned thing for them to attack. He went to check on Phang's condition, or was it because he wanted to be near Yu Li? He wasn't sure.

CHAPTER SEVENTEEN

Lon and his men rested in the outer chamber. The men were feeling a certain amount of pride at taking this small portion of the temple. They were resting and taking care of their wounds. Lon was pissed, not at his losses but at the fact that this mission, though seeming relatively simple at the outset, had turned into a full-scale police action.

He dismissed it from his mind, contemplating their immediate problem. So they have a machine gun? That altered the situation slightly, but he still had the upper hand. He would let his men rest, and then, shortly before dawn, when it was darkest, he would throw one last heavy attack into the room where they waited. They would not come out; of that he was certain. But he had enough troops to afford a number of casualties, and so they would wait and rest, as the foe was evidently doing. But their time was being wasted, the enemy. They had nowhere to go.

He went to a corner, had his aide lay out a blanket, curled up, and slept. But not before leaving orders that he was to be awakened at 5 A.M. sharp.

Casey waited also, not for the attack but for the hour when it would be darkest. Then they would make their escape. He went to one corner of the room and lay down behind a pile of fallen square-cut stones, laying his poncho and liner out and placing his head against the rocks. He closed his eyes. His mind was drifting away, when suddenly he felt a warmness beside him. Before he opened his eyes or could speak, Yu Li had picked up the poncho liner and covered them both with it. Still not speaking, she undid his trousers and deftly removed her own clothing without disturbing the liner covering them. Silently she moved closer to him, letting her skin rest on his. She put her mouth to his ear.

"You are my man, and I want to give you that which I have never given any man before you."

He pulled himself into a sitting position as Yu Li slid sideways to straddle his legs. Putting her hand between his legs, she grasped his manhood and gently placed him inside her moistness, just past the lips of her vagina.

He resisted the urge to thrust deep, holding back, feeling a strange excruciating pleasure in doing so. He knew that to penetrate her virginity by thrust would be painful. Taking a deep breath and relaxing, he put his arms about her and held her close until the initial sexual high had passed. Then he settled down, no longer feeling like he would burst inside.

Yu Li seemed to know that the initial crisis had passed. She moved herself slightly, adjusting her position, and gently moved herself down the full length of his throbbing muscle. She felt a sharp burning pain as her hymen broke and then an unfamiliar moistness inside. She lay still.

He didn't move, knowing what had happened. He must give her time. Then, as if on cue, they began to move together, their hips rotating in ever-widening small circles, thrusting as one and then stopping for a moment.

He gave her all the time she needed to adjust herself to this new invasion. He felt her right leg move up and back, around his waist, resting at the base of his spine. Her hips began to move with long sucking thrusts, pulling him forward and back, until he finally joined in a rhythm that grew stronger with each penetration, until Yu Li gave a long low cry under her breath and he felt a deep shudder of relief run its course through her body. He knew she had finished. She was complete now.

He moved her off him gently, the weight of her easy to

hoist and lay aside. Bending over her, he took one and then the other of her golden breasts into his mouth, kissing and sucking the nipples until they grew hard and eager for more. She threw her arms around him and held him tight, sobbing, holding him close, sweat dripping from her forehead, hair like a black cloud covering them both. She slept.

Damn, he thought, if those bastards out there had hit us a moment ago, I wouldn't even have noticed.

Waiting until Yu Li's breathing told him she was under, he bent to kiss her warm lips and then rose, arranging his clothes once again. This damned sure isn't in the military manuals, he thought, but it is good enough.

Yu Li snuggled into the warmth of the poncho liner, putting her face into the nylon, where she could still smell his body. She smiled a secret smile that only another woman could understand and fell asleep once again.

Casey moved to Van by the entrance. Van smiled at him, showing even white teeth. Casey pointed his finger at him.

"Van, this is one time I will not tolerate any damned wisecracks from you. Understand?"

Van nodded in agreement. "Of course, I understand, old boy. What do you think I am, an uncivilized savage? I was educated at Eton, remember? That puts me at least three rungs higher than you on the sensitivity ladder." Not giving Casey a chance to respond, Van asked, "When do we leave?"

"Soon! We'll give everyone a chance to rest. We may not get any more for a while. You take it easy and get some *pak* time. A siesta won't do you any harm, son. I'll cover things here for a bit; then we'll move 'em out."

Van moved over by George and in less than a minute's time was softly snoring. Casey smiled. Damn! They were good men. A warm feeling seemed to grab him. Maybe it was left over from Yu Li, but he felt exceptionally friendly and concerned for his friends tonight.

CHAPTER EIGHTEEN

It was quiet; the time was now. He moved quickly, waking his two men first and instructing them to rouse the Kamserai troops of Phang and prepare them to move out. Two of the Kams, healthy, stout-looking soldiers, were ordered to look after old Phang. Then he went personally to Phang's side and woke him.

"Old friend, it is time to leave. You go first."

Casey led them a short way through the temple, showing them the exit and telling them to go on ahead with Phang and the family. He and his two boys would follow shortly. He watched as they all crawled, winding their way through the tunnel and out into the open air, carrying their chief and then returning for Huan and Yu Li's mother. Casey went then to Van, instructing him to personally take care of Yu Li. Van started to protest but hesitated when he saw the steel determination in Casey's eyes.

Now there were only two remaining—he and George. Lon picked that exact moment to attack. Casey heard the sound of running feet in the hall, leading toward the room where he and George waited. Without hesitation, he turned the MG-34 to the hall and cut loose a long burst, moving the weapon deftly from side to side, laying down an impenetrable wall of small missiles. George stood beside him, loosing one bursting round after another into the hallway. The ear-shattering echo of their weapons was answered by the wailing screams of agony from the mouths of wounded and dying Khmer Rouge soldiers.

Casey's gun ran through a belt of fifty rounds. While George covered him, he reloaded. The Khmer were still coming, and as far as he was concerned, their return fire was getting too damned close for comfort. He could hear Lon urging his men on as he and George moved back toward the hole. Casey followed George into it and stopped firing, giving his man a chance to clear the tunnel. He could hear the Khmer soldiers running as they frantically searched the empty chambers, trying to locate them. The firing had stopped, and they were confused. But they were gradually getting oriented and had filled the room they'd just vacated. George yelled at him to hurry and join them outside.

Reaching into his jacket pocket, he removed a long gray object. It resembled a spray can of insecticide somewhat, but he knew that it was infinitely more deadly. A white phosphorus grenade could do a lot of damage anywhere, let alone inside a chamber such as the one he'd just left, packed tightly now with blind and groping combat troops.

Reaching into his other pocket, he removed another of the deadly grenades. He pulled the cotterlike retaining pins, holding the hammers down, waiting until the sounds told him that the room was jammed with men. Now! He tossed the two instruments of destruction into the room, one to the right and one to the left, spinning around. He'd better get his ass out of the area fast.

Before he reached the end of the tunnel, the WP grenades went off, ear-splitting, sending thousands of pieces of white burning death streaming throughout the room. For a second, the entire room was illuminated as if a huge flashbulb had exploded, freezing the Khmer soldiers in a variety of positions. Then the white death began reaching out for them in the enclosed area of the chamber. White phosphorus that burned as long as there was air to hit it. Large pieces burned their way into and through the soft, vulnerable flesh of several men's bodies and dropped onto the floor, still glowing white.

The battlewise ones quickly covered the white burning specks with dirt—anything to keep the air from getting to the phosphorus particles. The young had to suffer until the older men could come to their aid. When it was over, eight of Lon's men had been killed by the grenades. An additional nine were wounded from the phosphorus and would be unable to continue the chase. Another eight had been riddled to pieces by the fire from Casey and George's weapons in the hallway.

Lon was not a happy man when he located the escape route they had taken. For once disregarding his own safety, he threw himself into the tunnel and crawled through and out into the air. He ran to the edge of the swamp. Raising his AK-47, he snapped off one shot at a distant fleeing figure. The shadow of the figure dropped suddenly. Good, he thought. One for my side.

On his return trip through the snakelike tunnel, he was in less of a hurry. As he entered the chamber, he spotted the remains of Phang's man who had been downed by the snake and Phang's hand still grasping the head. That ought to slow them down a little, he figured. Gathering his men into some semblance of order, leaving the wounded to their own devices, he again set out in pursuit of his quarry.

Dawn found both parties wading through waist-deep water. Fog, forming from the cooler water meeting the warming air, nestled about their waists.

Casey counted. Out of the ten men Phang had had with him at the outset, there were now seven. Two had been killed, and one was unaccounted for.

George had heard a familiar noise several hours before but had said nothing to anyone. He knew the sound well. An Indochinese crocodile had made a kill. The gurgling, whishing sound had been the croc spinning itself around in the water, trying to tear bite-size pieces off its latest kill. What it could not eat now it would carry back to its lair under a mud island and wait for it to decay. It would be easier to eat then. Casey had noted that one of Phang's men was missing. He had to be the croc's meal. George shuddered. That was a hell of a way for a man to die. He continued to march.

All that day and all night they waded, occasionally finding some semidry land to walk on for a while. But the scout they had placed at their rear would always come running at the moment they decided to try to rest, saying that the Khmer were close behind. They had to keep moving.

The killing pace began to take its toll on the women and on old Phang, wounded as he was. Casey took Yu Li under his arm and helped her forward, counting each step, assuring her that they would be out of the swamp soon. Huan helped his wife, and the Kamserai took turns aiding their chief. They all kept moving, taking one clogging, mud-sucking step at a time. Finally, when they were all certain they could go no farther, Casey's promise that they'd soon be out came true. He looked down at his feet and realized that he'd been walking on dry ground for some time without knowing it. Not damp ground but land that was completely and thoroughly dry. They were out of the swamp. He couldn't believe it. He must have been in a stupor and unaware that he had been. He shook his head to clear it and slowly let Yu Li slide down his arm until she touched the ground.

Casey called to George, not loud, more a harsh whisper. "Take a couple of the Kamserai and fix a Malay gate for our friends behind us, son."

George grunted. The closest he ever came to an expression of pleasure was just then, Casey thought. George sat about gathering the help he needed in preparing the gate to Casey's specifications. He'd done them before; and he knew how his main man liked them set.

A wooden log with sharpened stakes tied across its width so that when the rope, or trip wire, was sprung, the log bar would swing down and the stakes would strike whoever had tripped the trap, embedding the stakes deep in the chest or stomach, depending on the person's height. It wasn't pleasant to think about, but George enjoyed preparing it. It took a mere fifteen minutes to set up and was usually well worth the effort in casualties.

Casey knew that Yu Li and her kin, especially her mother, needed this well-deserved rest period. He was glad to offer it to them, though he dreaded the results of the wasted time.

He walked over to where the two Kamserai warriors had placed Phang on the ground. The old man was hanging on like a trooper but didn't look good to Casey.

"Old one, it is time for us to part company. I'm going to send you and your men back into the swamp. You can exit somewhere on the other side, and your men can take you home. You've all done more than your share. Me and my two boys can take it the rest of the way now. We're only a couple of hours away from the Kampot River. When we get there, we'll grab a junk sampan and head for the coast."

Phang grunted in protest, but Casey shook his head. "No, Phang, you could do us no more good there, especially in your condition now. You belong in the woods with your people."

Phang started to complain again, weak but determined. Casey wouldn't hear it. He knelt down closer to the old warrior, tasting salty tears at the corner of his mouth as he hugged his aged friend gently.

"Long life and many sons for you, Chief of the Kamserai."

Casey's Adam's apple threatened to choke him as he spoke. He motioned for the warriors to take their chief back the way they'd just come. Back into the swamp, knowing that his pursuers would more than likely follow the signs that would lead them to the party accompanying the women, away from Phang and his men. The old one and his troops would be safe.

They moved out, leaving Casey and his small party

alone. Phang's eyes were dim but still alert yet clouded with real regret at leaving his American warrior friend.

Casey turned determinedly to his two-man squad, grinning. "Well, gentlemen, it looks like we're all that's left now. Let's move out. Check your weapons while we move."

They did as he instructed, cleaning the muck and scum from the working parts of their arms, making them as battle-ready as possible without breaking them down completely.

They reentered the jungle of the lowlands. They were in the basin country of Cambodia now, only a few feet above sea level, winding and twisting their way, each taking a turn at the point position. Casey occasionally caught Yu Li's eye, and the memory of the events of the previous evening flashed on him again, despite his fatigue.

They had not quite reached the river when Lon's men located the position from which Casey's small party had first exited the swamp. The Meo tracker was eager to get on their trail, but one of Lon's noncoms, eager to show his own skills, ordered the Meo to go back, telling him that he would personally take point. The overly eager sergeant spent about ten minutes in the lead position, urging himself and his followers forward. Suddenly four sharpened stakes swung down from the trees, burying themselves so deeply in the man's belly that their points exited his back, keeping him hanging there screaming. Lon came forward, shooting the man in the head to end his misery and the warning noise his throat was making.

The Meo tracker reported that the ones they were following had split up. Some, he told his colonel, had gone back into the swamp, but the women and the American were in front of them.

Lon squinted doubtfully. "How do you know the American is in front of us? How can you be sure?"

The Meo pointed to the damp earth and a boot imprint in the moistness of it, placing his own foot beside it. It was obvious that a much larger man had passed this way. Lon was furious that he himself had not seen it.

"Good! Every man on his feet and back on the trail. After the American and his party. Let the Kamserai coward dogs go. We want no more of the waters of that swamp. May the beasts rot in it. I want the American."

Lon whipped his men forward after the shadows of Casey and his party.

Gambling an hour, Casey allowed Yu Li and her mother to rest awhile, sleeping under the watchful eyes of Van and George. Yu Li's father used the time to prepare food for them all. Cold rice, foul-tasting from the waters of the swamp that had seeped into the plastic wrappings, was all they had. The women woke. Grain by small grain, Huan fed the rice carefully to his exhausted wife, placing small bites between her lips, encouraging her to eat with a combination of endearments and insincere threats. Yu Li ate without speaking and laid her head to the ground again. With one deep sigh she was gone, sound asleep again. Casey was glad she was able to rest. She damned sure needed it.

He moved on ahead. He didn't see it! He smelled it! The river, he thought. Damnit, it was the river. He could smell the bastard. He broke through the reeds barring his way. There it was, the way home. Follow its course and we've got it made.

Checking his compass against the map, he saw that they were close to the line of flight of the Chinese Nationalist aircraft, which, if there were no hitches in their plan, was due overhead tonight. Now they had more than just a chance. Had it been only three nights since they'd left the DZ? Damn! It seemed like three weeks.

George came up behind him, startling Casey back to awareness. At first Casey thought that something must be wrong for his man to have come after him. He spoke quickly.

"Is everything okay back there? What's wrong?"

George put up his hand, nodding that all was fine. At the same moment, from behind them, came a long burst of automatic rifle fire from an AK. The deeper answering fire from Van's G-3 stopped when several other weapons opened up.

He felt the rush of fear spreading over him, not fear for himself but for Yu Li and the others. They've been captured or, worse, killed! Starting to curse George, he stopped short, realizing that even had he been there, he could probably have done little. A flash of guilt set in. George jerked his arm, pulling him to the ground, bringing him back from the guilt.

"Easy, Trung Si, easy! We must take things slow and see what we may see. If the gods are kind, we may yet do what we came to this land to do."

Casey got his thoughts back into perspective, knowing that George was right. Silently they crouched and moved out, blending into the high grass, taking the utmost care to leave no signs behind.

"They must still have the Meo tracker with them, Trung Si. It would be wise to remove him. He has caused us enough trouble, wouldn't you agree?"

Casey nodded in agreement, and George slithered away from him into the high grass.

The Meo was sniffing the trail not fifty meters from where they'd just captured the Viet, the Chinese, and his women. His colonel wanted the American, and he was determined to find him for his leader. The Meo bent over, his eyes drawn, his nose close to the earth. Like Egyptian hieroglyphics, strange figures were freshly etched into the claylike soil. He studied them, speaking softly to himself, muttering: "What do these scratches mean? Why are they here?"

A steel arm went around his throat as George answered his question. "They are there to let you know you are dead, Meo traitor!"

George slid his blade beneath the last rib on the Meo's

right side, moving the cold steel in and slicing to the left. He severed the tracker's spinal cord. Then there was a quick upward movement, and the steel entered the large artery, allowing a flow of blood into the abdominal cavity. In less than four seconds the Meo was unconscious and paralyzed, bleeding to death internally. George had learned that particular cut from an Algerian in the legion. Algerians were good with blades.

Returning to Casey's side, he informed him that the tracker would cause them no more problems. "Now, Trung Si, how do we get Van and the Chinese family back into our possession?"

Casey thought about it. "How many of them would you say are left, George? We took out a good number of them. There should be no more than twenty."

George nodded as Casey continued. "They wouldn't expect us to hit them this soon. With the .34 we should be able to even up the odds a little more. They will probably figure us to hit them at night, if at all, so let's do the unexpected and look them over now. If it looks good, we'll burn their asses right now and make a run for the river. Without their Meo to track for them, we might just have a pretty good chance to make it. What do you say, little buddy?"

George grunted. It really made no difference to him whether they hit them now or later tonight. Heavy thinking was not his fort. He would leave all that to Trung Si gladly.

Moving silently, they returned to the edge of the small clearing where they'd left the others a short time before. George made his way quickly up a tree and looked the situation over while Casey covered him. Sliding down with a style that strongly resembled that of a cheetah, he told Casey what he had viewed from above.

"Twenty-two men to my count, Trung Si. The Khmer have only five or six posted as guards. We can easily bypass them and take out the two on our side. The others are gathered around their colonel, who is busy showing off his prisoners to his men and making a speech on his successful mission.''

"Okay, George. That's great. Where are the two sentries that, as you say, are on our side?"

George quickly outlined their direction, and Casey made his decision. "All right, George, here's what we'll do. You take the one on the left, and I'll take out the one by the treestump."

Slinging his .34 to his back, he and George slid into the grass, each making his own way toward his target, a target that waited unknowingly for death. The Khmer were not concerned about a counterattack. They were used to being the hunter, not the hunted.

The young Khmer by the treestump was daydreaming about his tender thirteen-year-old who waited for his return to their home village as Casey's knife opened his windpipe, letting the air escape from his lungs. He drowned in his own blood while Casey counted the rounds he had remaining and loaded his MG.

"Four belts of fifty rounds each," he said almost too loudly to himself. "That should do it for now."

Waiting for George to complete his kill, he advanced to the edge of the tall grass and waited, belly to the damp ground, his eyes taking in the entire scene before him, mentally calculating the position of everyone.

Van was on his knees before the leader of the Khmer soldiers. Casey immediately recognized the insignia of rank on the officer.

"A colonel! So that's the bastard chasing us and screaming at the top of his lungs," he whispered to himself.

One of the colonel's men had Van by the hair, forcing his head to the rear while the officer interrogated him. He could see that Van had been hit. A round had clipped him through his trapezius. Now that the man had twisted Van's head around, Casey could see that another had hit him in the cheek, fracturing the zygoma. He could hear the colonel informing Van what would become of him and what he would let his men do to the women if Van refused to tell him what he wanted to hear.

A small cough told Casey that George had finished his mission. Holding his hand slightly up in the air and grinning, George proudly showed him the trophy he'd taken from his kill—a small, yellow, bloodstained ear. Casey grunted in disgust and pointed to the position of Yu Li and her family.

"Get them over to me when the shooting starts. Van still looks in good enough shape to take care of himself. You get close to Yu Li and wait for me to kick off the action. Got it?"

George nodded, fading back into the brush. Moments later, he gave Casey the high sign that he was in position, close to the girl and her family, waiting for Casey's next move.

Instinctive moves would take over now, Casey knew. He drew a deep breath, let it out, and drew another, holding it in for only a second. He aimed at the bulk of the Khmer troops, gathered near their colonel in a cluster, watching intently their glorious leader's action with Van.

The MG fired without his even realizing exactly when the trigger had been pulled, shattering the silence of the moment. Again, the familiar feel of the gun throbbing against him made itself known, as the 7.62 NATO-type rounds whipped their way through the packed bodies of the Khmer Rouge, flesh giving easily against the flying metal. He used the burning of the tracers to follow the paths his bullets took, moving the gun to the group situated around Van, sighting head-high so as not to hit his own man. He let loose with a long hosing burst that sent all in the vicinity diving for cover. As they dove, Van straightened, giving the Khmer who had been holding his hair a swift, accurate kick to the throat, fracturing the man's esophagus and leaving him to choke to death. Van raced to the sound of the MG's fire and threw himself to the ground beside Casey.

George had by this time grabbed Yu Li, motioning to her mother and father, and the four of them had pulled quickly back into the edge of the clearing and out of the Khmer's sight. The soldiers were presently too concerned with their own safety to be looking for the captives. They raced in all directions toward the safety of the brush, trying to escape the bright streaks of death that flew around them.

At their head was Colonel Lon. He ran until he stumbled and fell to the ground, knocking the wind from his burning lungs. His body was shaking from fear. That was too close, he thought. He had almost been killed. The idea of being killed was almost more than he could bear.

Casey moved his piece from side to side, spraying the edges of the clearing, keeping the Khmer in confusion with their heads hugging the ground inside the high grass. Van raced back into the clearing and retrieved his weapon along with the Swedish "K" the Khmer had dropped in their haste to put some distance between themselves and these foreign beasts who didn't play fair.

When he returned to Casey's position and they had reunited with George and Yu Li's family, they wasted no time heading for the river. Entering the cool water, they stayed close to the edge, losing themselves in the reeds, letting the current carry them slowly downriver. They moved in this manner until darkness set in and then moved to land, shivering from cold and exhaustion. The three mercenaries dried their weapons as best they could and motioned for the family to follow. Together, they moved as one through the small willows and brush by the water's edge, passing several small boats, their owners resting or repairing their nets for the next excursion. Finally, Van pointed to one that seemed somewhat larger than the rest and unattended. But was it? The family or crew were more than likely already asleep inside. From all appearances, though, it had exactly what the six of them would need. An outboard motor was visible in the shadows, and the sampan looked in great shape, about thirty-five feet in length, with one large square sail. Probably as good as they'd find, Casey surmised.

They waited in hiding until all the fires by the water's edge had died out. Casey sent George, along with Huan's family, downstream to wait and watch for them. They would reunite when he and Van had successfully taken the boat. Although Van was hurting, he hadn't complained. He was carrying no lead, and Casey figured he'd make it all right. The tough bastard had caught worse before, Casey knew, and the quicker he got him on the boat, the quicker he could rest up.

Gently, the two of them slid into the river. He seemed as light as a feather suddenly from the buoyancy of the water and the change in his body temperature. Van had taken his MG with him, not wanting to chance losing it. The loss of its burdensome weight alone was enough to make a man feel a hell of a lot freer.

Letting the current sweep them along, they finally bumped into the boat, smelling the wet wood and foul pitch that was used for caulking. They eased along the side of the craft to its rear. An anchor line held the boat in position there, and they used it to haul themselves silently aboard. Goose bumps whipped over Casey as a slight breeze cooled the wetness of his clothing. He heard a small cough from inside the cabin and realized that he'd been correct in assuming that the craft was occupied. He made his way down the side of the deck to the sound of the cough.

Taking his K-bar out of its scabbard, he eased through the opening to the cabin and to the side of the sleeping figure. He put its point to the throat of the man occupying the bunk. The Cambode opened his eyes as Casey shushed him, his knife's point warning him to be still and silent, making itself known from the slight and sharp pain at his throat. His eyes, Casey could see in the dim moonlight, were wide with fear. Casey motioned for him to rise and wake the others. From where Casey crouched, the two other figures appeared to be a woman and child. Holding the knife steadily on the man, he allowed him to bend over the woman, speaking softly and shaking her gently. The fisherman whispered softly to her, explaining the situation. The woman rose and picked up her sleeping child. Together, they moved outside, where Casey motioned for them to get off the boat. The man seemed more than eager to do as he was instructed, glad to learn that they were not to be killed. It was bad enough to lose one's boat, but one's life was something else.

Once they were on land, Van cut loose the bowline, freeing the craft from its anchor and allowing the sampan to float free and into the current. Then Van released the stern anchor, and they were in the river, moving silently downstream and away from the shore. Using the tiller and a long oar pole, Casey guided the craft downriver, quickly moving to shore when he saw George waving from the bank. Quickly, George and the family boarded the sampan. Once they were all on deck, Casey headed the boat into midstream again in the direction of the coast. All that night they traveled downriver.

The following morning he moved inside, allowing Van, George, and the Orientals to appear as a fishing family. His Occidental round eyes would definitely cause suspicion if seen.

They passed town after town, many built on stilts and piles by the river. Van and Yu Li waved nonchalantly at the villagers as they passed by. They rested that night under the shelter of the cabin. Yu Li came to him again, unashamed at the presence of her parents, and slept in his arms. It was pleasant having her there near him. The tenseness of the action of the past few days slowly left his body, and he too rested.

Casey heard a familiar sound, a throbbing that was gradually increasing in tempo. Raising his eyes, he was still unable to see it, but overhead somewhere, hidden in the clouds, he knew that a plane was looking for them, searching for the party below, waiting to take them out of here and to safety. The cloud cover was preventing the aircraft from seeing them, and there was not a damn thing he or anyone else could do to correct the situation.

Xin loy, he thought (sorry about that). What else could he do? He rolled over to face Yu Li and slept, letting the rolling waters of the Kampot rock them gently in their sleep, allowing the river to move them each minute closer to the coast and safety.

CHAPTER NINETEEN

Colonel Lon was not sleeping, however. He was highly pissed. He was making his way downriver in a commandeered truck along with his best troops who had survived the skirmish with the American dog and his people. He had only eight men left now, but they would do for the remainder of his mission.

By radio, he informed higher headquarters that all was in order, that several of the invaders had been killed, and that more had been driven across the border into Vietnam. Also, would headquarters please notify their Viet brothers in socialism that a unit of Kamserai was presently heading south toward the Iron Triangle?

Lon had long since questioned the fisherman and his family whose boat the American had stolen. He gained what details he could from them and then headed his men downstream in hot pursuit. Sometime that night, unknown to him and his men as well as to Casey and his crew, the colonel had passed the sampan's location in the darkness. Lon could not tell headquarters the truth about what this mission, simple as it had seemed from the outset, had cost them all and how he still had nothing to show them for that loss. After all, if he caught them in the end, he could easily justify the cost.

Driving all through the night, Lon stopped at each large village, telling the cadre in charge to be on the alert and to send word ahead to him if they spotted the craft. They were not to attempt to stop it themselves, nor would they fire on it. That pleasure would be his alone.

Lon's truck pulled into the town of Prey Nop. He dismounted and went directly to a small motorized river patrol unit. After identifying himself, he immediately pulled rank and issued orders personally to the unit. He did, however, inform the gunboat commander that he would be highly rewarded for his cooperation in this security matter. The captain, sensing that something important was in the wind, agreed with the colonel. After all, he was outranked. If anything went awry in the operation, it would be the colonel's ass, not his.

Toward dawn, the word that Lon had been impatiently awaiting finally came to him. The sampan had been spotted and should arrive at their area by dusk the same day. Lon told the captain that they would not wait and instead would surprise them upstream. The gunboat's commander shook his head, adamantly explaining that the river was mostly uncharted and had many treacherous shallows and sandbars. His vessel drew too much water to risk it. It would be much better to wait for them and intercept them about three miles farther downriver, where the channel narrowed. There they could easily spot any passing boat, even in the darkness. Lon didn't relish getting stuck on an upstream sandbar, though he hated delays of any kind. But he reluctantly agreed to do as the captain had suggested. The boat headed downriver to the narrows, its engines throbbing smoothly.

The captain called down to the engine room, where his only mechanic tended to the engines assigned to his care. The precision motors were his pride and joy: good efficient engines from the United States. He treated them like tiny babies.

The gunboat arrived at the desired position. The crew immediately dropped the bow anchor and faced the craft upstream, where they could watch for oncoming boats. They waited.

Casey and his slight crew were relaxing, enjoying this

chance to rest and eat. The boat was well stocked with fish and rice. He tried to figure their odds. Here on the river they were relatively safe. One more night and they would be in the clear. So far, so good. If luck stayed with them, they'd be out of this hellhole tomorrow. It might be better, though, he thought, if they moved to land for a while and then back to the river. He didn't like holding one position for so long. But the women had walked enough and would probably not be able to make it on foot. They were getting farther into heavily populated areas now, and his pale eyes and brown hair would stand out like red flags. No, the river was more than likely their best shot.

Again, night began to settle on them, growing darker as they passed each village. One more down, how many more to go? he would mentally calculate as they floated past each town.

As they passed Kampong, he raised the cabin tarp and looked out. From where he was, he could see a group of men gathered at the pier. They looked more like soldiers than fishermen, and there were no boats around. That was neither good nor bad, though. If they were soldiers waiting to spot them going by, without boats they could not give chase. However, they could send word downstream to whomever waited below. Too late to worry about that now. Hell with it. If they waited downriver, there was little Casey could do about it, anyway. He would wait until the situation came up to decide what to do.

They passed the town, and Van steered the sampan out of the current and over to the river's edge as far as he dared, using the shoreline to hide the craft as much as possible.

George moved to the bow, looking ahead to check for sandbars or stumps. A single shot rang out, dropping George as if he'd been poleaxed.

Lon turned quickly to the young sailor who'd fired, stunned at the man's stupidity in warning the oncoming boat. The colonel pulled his pistol from his holster and at point-blank range shot the man in the face. The captain started to protest, but the expression on Lon's face said that he'd be better off keeping his mouth shut.

"The young fool gave us away, Captain. Start your engines and let's get after them," he screamed.

The captain gave the order. The engines roared to life, and busy sailors hoisted anchor.

When George fell, Casey ran to his side. Seeing that he'd been hit in the face, he called for Yu Li to help. While she looked after George, he raced to the stern and helped Huan start the outboard motor. Sputtering, the small engine kicked into life, and they pulled away, keeping to the side of the river.

They passed the narrows and entered a wide channel with many outlets and avenues, crossing over water so shallow that the outboard motor threw up clouds of mud.

Damn, he thought, come on darkness, it's our only chance. He watched as Yu Li and her mother bandaged George's face, covering both eyes.

The gunboat's engines were roaring. The searchlight was frantically moving across the water in its forward path, reaching out and probing the darkness in the direction of the sampan. Lon urged the captain and his crew on. Just then, the light picked up the sampan ahead of them, and he ordered the ship to fire on it. They did as he'd ordered. Round after round, 20-mm shells smashed the planks of the small vessel's hull. But it still was not enough to sink it. The tiny outboard motor pushed the sampan on. Lon yelled at the captain when he decided they'd given their best effort and would give up the chase. Lon knocked him down with a sweep of his arm and took the wheel himself, promptly running the gunboat onto a sandbar, watching helplessly as the battered sampan made its way downstream.

The ocean and safety, Lon knew, was less than twenty miles away. By dawn, the American and his people would be outside the limits of his Cambodian authority. In a rage he went to the deck gun and grabbed its trigger. Swinging the big weapon around in the direction of the fading sampan, he emptied the magazine in a high flying arc. It was out of the searchlight's range now, but one round found its way blindly to the deck and exploded, sending several pieces of half-dollar-sized shards of metal flying around. One of these hit Huan slightly above the groin. The hot steel cooled off inside him as he slipped wordlessly into a welcome unconsciousness.

A sound of mourning came from Huan's women. Casey hissed loudly for them to be quiet. Their sound would guide their followers. The women chocked back their grief and bandaged his wound.

He left Van at the wheel and knelt beside Huan. Checking him over carefully, he located another smaller entry point just below the right pectoral. He knew that the wounds were damned serious. Without proper treatment for at least the lower injury, peritonitis would soon set in.

All that night they sailed, killing the outboard, maintaining silence, and taking their time. If they were not careful, they could get stuck like the gunboat. At least that's what he had assumed had happened to them, since there was no further chase.

The sun had been up for several hours when a change in the wind gained his attention. There was a new smell, different from the dankness of the dark river water's odor. The ocean! They had at last arrived at the ocean.

Raising the ragged sail, he and Van worked their small craft into the light breakers. Soon they were in the South China Sea and on their way home. Slowly, relentlessly, the sampan made its way against the tide, trying desperately to hold them back and prevent them from entering new waters. Foot by short foot, they moved gradually forward until they were out and clear of the pull from the shore's currents. The tiny ship moved away, leaving behind it the shore and coastline of Cambodia fading into the horizon. Only Casey watched this happen; the others were lying about on the deck in varying degrees of exhaustion.

Yu Li lay curled up in a fetal knot at his feet. He guarded the tiller, guiding the sampan sluggishly through the waters of the sea, taking bearings occasionally with his compass for a heading on Malaya. It was closer than the Phillipines, and Malaya was home.

Van tossed restlessly in his tormented sleep, his thin and frail frame exhausted from the long run. The wound on his head looked worse than it actually was, Casey thought. As long as they could prevent infection, he shouldn't have any more than a handsome new scar to show his girl friends. George, though, he guessed, might be a different ballgame. He would go to check on him as soon as Van woke and relieved him.

Yu Li's mother slept in what was left of the shelter area on the deck of the boat, covering herself with her man's shirt. They should reach one of the Malay islands, he calculated, no later than the next morning if the wind and the weather held for them. They had made it. It was all over.

Casting one last look behind, he squinted his eyes against the reflected glare of the setting sun. A speck on the horizon behind them suddenly appeared, growing larger as he stared.

"No! Damnit to hell! It's not fair. We beat them. We won! They can't take us now. We're outside their limits," he shouted aloud. But even as he thought about it, he was well aware that if they could, they damned sure would take them back.

The captain of the gunboat in pursuit had been given very specific orders: Bring them back! Dead or alive, but bring them back. The gunboat sped up, closing the gap between them and the shot-up sampan. He was moving damned fast.

Casey quickly assessed their position. They were damned near out of ammo; not enough to fight with and most assuredly nothing heavy enough to handle that gunboat. Shit! From this distance he could already see the Bofors mounted on their deck. That cuts it! They can blow us away with no sweat at all. George is out of the fight. The head wound wouldn't allow him to live twenty-four hours in one of their filthy rotten jails if any of us survived long enough to even make it to one of their jails, he quickly added in his mind. And what of Yu Li and her mother? What would lie ahead for them?

Yu Li woke just then, her eyes following his determined gaze, spotting the communist gunship, now closing fast. With her female intuition, she knew exactly what was going through his mind. She pulled herself up from the deck and to his side, laying her head on his leg and speaking softly. "We fought them well, did we not, my love?"

He nodded without speaking, stroking her hair with one knotted, scarred hand. She took his free hand and kissed it gently, ignoring the dirt and dried blood.

"We should not stop fighting them. Is it not better to die here and now than to perish a little bit at a time as they may choose? I know these beasts. Let us take them with us if we can, or at least as many as possible. I would not have you give me or yourself to them."

He motioned to her mother, sleeping on deck. "And what of her? And my men? Am I to be responsible for all your deaths?"

Yu Li shook her head. "Without my father, she has no real life left to her. Her babies are safe. She will die bravely."

Casey noticed that Van's eyes were open. "Did you hear what the little one said, old friend?"

Van coughed, clearing his throat. "She is right. To allow them to take us alive would be more than stupid, old boy. Let us end our mission on our own terms."

Casey looked over at Huan. Somehow he had pulled himself into a sitting position against the side of the wrecked cabin. He motioned to Van, who went to the Chinese man's side, bending over low and speaking in Chinese. He turned to Casey.

"He understands the situation. He says to kill the communist bastards."

"Kill them." Huan coughed weakly, specks of bloody

film bubbling on his lips, giving evidence that the lungs
had been hit.

"Okay! That's the way it will be, then. What do we
have left to hit them with, though? That's the damned
question. Should we maybe throw the friggin' sail at them?"
Casey asked bitterly.

Van did a fast inventory. They had one magazine remaining for the Swedish "K" and four 9-mm mags to be
divided equally between the two pistols—Van's P-38 and
George's Browning—plus four grenades. Not an arsenal
by any means.

Van leaned over again to take Huan's pistol. Huan
whispered in his ear, and Van grinned slowly, nodding in
the affirmative.

"What did he say that would crack you up at a time like
this?" Casey queried.

"He does not wish to die without taking some of them
with him, Sergeant. He would like two of the grenades for
himself."

He agreed with the man's request. "Why the hell not?
We all started this thing together, and we'll finish it the
same way. Give the brave little man what he wants." He
looked back at the boat coming on them. He could read the
lettering on the hull.

"Now listen, each of you. This is the way we'll play it.
We just might be able to take a few of the bastards out
before they blow us out of the sea. Yu Li, you stand
behind me with the SMG. When they slow to board us,
assuming they don't blow us out of the water first, I'll
show them empty hands. While you're behind me, pull the
pins on the grenades hanging on my belt in the back. Hand
them to me damned fast when I tell you to."

She nodded, and he turned to Van. "Take that bandage
off your head and break the wound open again. Get some
blood flowing. I want you to look like you've had your
damned brains blown out. Lay down close to the side of
the sampan. When I toss the grenades on their ship, use

the side for cover and pepper the hell out of 'em with your pistol.''

He turned again to Yu Li. "As soon as I throw the grenades, I'll drop. You let loose with the 'K.' I'll take out whoever I can with my pistol. Both of you, and you too, Huan, remember to save a little ammo.''

Each of them knew what he meant. The last rounds would be used on any of them whom the reds didn't get. Huan nodded, as did the rest, and pulled himself up to take a drink from a can near him. Casey stopped him.

"Don't, Huan! That's gasoline. Here, drink this.'' He handed him his own canteen. "I know you're not supposed to drink with that gut wound you've got, but what the hell. We don't have much of a life expectancy left right now.''

The gunboat was within hailing distance now, and it slowed, its wake jostling the smaller craft. The weapon on the bow spit out several rounds over the bow of the sampan, and they waited to see if the Americans would respond with fire of their own.

When no fire was returned, Lon showed himself at the bow and called to them in good English. "It is all over for you. Now you will surrender to me, all of you. None shall be harmed. You will be given a fair trial, and the ones you have kidnaped shall be returned to their homes. Do you hear me, American? Do you understand?''

Casey yelled back, deciding that he'd better give the colonel a little food for thought. "I hear you! But listen! Do you swear that we will be given fair trials and the women will go free?''

"Yes, American. You have my word. The word of a respected and trustworthy officer. We have no war against women. All we want is for you and your outlaws to surrender and face justice in a public trial. Then the entire world will know how America tries to overthrow the rightful government of a peaceful nation in the name of her democracy. Surrender and stand trial. Perhaps you will be shown leniency if you testify that you are merely a stooge for the CIA. Stand up now and show yourselves. You will not be harmed."

Casey rose with Yu Li erect and directly behind him. His huge frame was hiding most of her, he hoped. He called to the gunboat, now almost onside: "I'm the only man who can stand. The others are either shot up badly or dead."

He raised his hands, clasping them behind his head in what looked like the proper POW method. He whispered under his breath, not moving his lips. "Get ready, Yu Li. I love you."

She moved even closer to him, whispering, her firm young breasts touching his back. "We are together. It is enough for me."

The Khmer crew were tossing grappling lines to the deck of the pathetic little sampan that had performed so nobly for her crew of refugees.

"Now, Yu Li," he hissed.

She pulled the pins on the two grenades held next to her skin and handed them, one in each hand, around Casey's waist. His hands came quickly from behind his neck and dropped down, grasping the two steel balls of death. He threw them to the deck of the gunboat, dropping to the deck at the same instant. Yu Li raised the Swedish "K" and cut loose with a long hosing burst that sent Khmer sailors falling into the water. The sight of the grenades in midair, heading in their direction, was the only thing that the ship's commander and Colonel Lon had eyes for. Their men were no different. They all ducked for cover. Before the two grenades had landed on deck, Van was already up and trying to blow the captain away. His close misses had aided the officer in his desire to seek cover fast. Lon was already in hiding below the deck's edge when the grenades went off, blasting several Khmers into clots of jelly.

Before the crew of the gunboat could react, Casey saw Huan throwing himself into the smoke rising from the deck of the gunboat, carrying the can of gasoline. He was screaming at the top of his lungs in his madness, a choking scream from blood-filled lungs.

He leaped onto the deck of the enemy ship like an Asiatic Errol Flynn, throwing himself through an open hatch and into the engine room below deck. An amazed Khmer sailor watched in astonishment at the fearful-looking apparition that had suddenly appeared before him. What was this bloody-looking figure that was carrying a gas can? What were his intentions? "No! No! Sweet Buddha, no!"

Huan landed catlike, raised himself up, and smiled at the startled sailor. He laughed wildly, pulling the pins on the two grenades Van had given him.

On the deck above, action had ceased temporarily. All were stunned by what had so suddenly occurred. A weak laugh came to their ears from below, and, shortly following the mad laugh, a tremendous explosion tore the belly out of the Khmer vessel.

"White phosphorus," Casey yelled to Van. "You gave him the white phosphorous grenades!"

The white heat from the grenades set off the gas can that Huan was carrying, which in turn ignited the fuel tanks of the gunboat, sinking the vessel in less than a minute.

Casey, Van, Yu Li, and her frail, surprised mother stood watching the bubbling water. Pieces of debris were now breaking free and rising to the surface. Casey recognized what was left of the colonel's uniform as it floated to the top. There was very little of the man inside of it. He and two others were all that came up as they watched. The rest were at the bottom by now, and if Huan's religion was right, he would never lack for servants in the next life.

George still lay blissfully asleep on the deck, unaware of what had just transpired.

Seeing that all on board were unharmed, Casey moved closer to the side and yelled to the few survivors Yu Li had knocked from the decks with her first burst. They were wounded but still alive. After what they'd just seen, he knew that they were probably thanking their gods that they'd been hit first. They were hanging on to planks that had surfaced, yelling to him for mercy.

"I'm not going to kill you men. Over there is your country." He pointed to the unseen shore. "Make it if you can. You are all on your own."

As he turned back to his own passengers, his eyes suddenly sighted beneath the dark waters a gray torpedolike shape making ever tighter circles of its prey. A white-tipped shark, drawn by the scent of fresh blood, made his presence known by one quick flash of his dorsal fin above the water. As the dark deadly shape disappeared from sight, Casey turned to Van.

"You knew exactly what Huan intended to do, didn't you?"

Van nodded, his eyes dropping. "Yes, I knew. But it was what he wanted. I didn't have the heart to deny him that right."

"You did what you had to, my friend," Casey said, patting Van on the back.

Van suddenly grinned, throwing up his arms. "What do we do now, old chap? Shall we go home and purchase us a pub or what?"

Casey shook his head in disbelief. "No, Van, I don't think we would enjoy doing that for the rest of our lives."

Van sighed with relief. "Good! I was afraid you might want to settle down. Listen, my friend, we three have a few things in common. One is that we are very good at what we do, I mean, soldiering. Now, with the money the old Chinese will pay us, we can afford our own army. Let us find the best and pick the wars we want to fight. When and where we choose. What is life, anyway? Let us, like Huan, pick our time and place to die, like real men."

Yu Li looked at her man, knowing now that he was not hers, that he could never be hers. He belonged to war as much as anything belonged to anything. He was a warrior.

Casey set sail again, on course for Malaya. He was physically guiding the small ship, but his mind was else-where. Van didn't know how right he was about Casey and wars. The Hebrew, Jesus, had seen to this soldier's plight long ago, in a land far from where they were now. *Soldier, you are content with what you are, then that you shall remain until we meet again.*

The words echoed in Casca's tormented mind. *Where was He? When would He come again? Where will He send me next?*